What Dwells Beneath The Waves

Robbie Dorman

What Dwells Beneath The Waves by Robbie Dorman

© 2021 Robert Dorman. All rights reserved.

www.robbiedorman.com

ISBN-13: 978-1-7336388-8-3

Cover design by Bukovero

This is a work of fiction. All characters and events portrayed in this book are fictitious and any resemblance to real people or events is purely coincidental.

No part of this book may be reproduced, stored in a retrieval system, or transmitted in any form or by any means, including mechanical, electric, photocopying, recording, or otherwise, without the prior written permission of the publisher.

For Edgar.

1

Moira felt the water beneath her, its unyielding and incredible size, its depth and power. She felt it, and it hurt.

The AC blasted through the rented hatchback, doing its best to keep out the oppressive South Florida heat. Moira's small frame usually made sure she felt cold, but not today, not here. The sun was too close here, and the tired AC couldn't keep up. Her black Misfits shirt stuck to her damp skin. She pushed the button on the controls one more time, hoping that somehow it would make the air blow harder and cooler. It did nothing, but Moira should probably thank the half-functioning AC for its distraction, the distraction from the water.

It spread out in every direction from US 1, a few feet of concrete keeping her car from it. A thin skein of bridge delineated between the water of the Gulf and of the Atlantic, the Seven Mile Bridge keeping them contained and organized and labeled correctly. Moira would keep those thoughts on top, of pedantry and metaphor. She would try to keep them on top, and keep the desperate lagoon of fear below, far below, deep inside, so deep even the tips of her toes wouldn't drag along the surface, just as the tires of her car kept off the water by the aging concrete poured decades ago as man did their best to reach the scattered islands of the Florida Keys.

It wasn't very deep, she knew. At some points she could get out and walk, but she kept that thought away as well, because even being close to that tremendous yawning void of deep, dark water made her stomach ache and her throat close.

"You think you can handle it?"

She had been sitting at her desk in New York. Martin Englehart stood nearby, drinking his coffee slowly, even as it burnt his tongue.

"You know, you can wait for it to cool before you drink it," she said.

"But then it'd be cold," said Martin. "You're trying to change the subject. I can handle the Keys if you want, and you can do the crab fishermen in Maryland."

"I picked it for a reason," said Moira, breaking eye contact with him, looking at her screen, staring at pictures of green islands floating on an ocean of blue, thin strands of concrete connecting them. She arrowed through them.

"Yeah, because you're allergic to showing any kind of vulnerability," said Martin.

"That's not true," said Moira.

"Do your parents know you're going down there?"

"No," said Moira. "And I'm not going to tell them. They worry enough about me already."

"Fair enough. I will *happily* trade with you, it's not a problem," said Martin.

"You just want a vacation," said Moira.

"South Florida is miserable in the summer," said Martin. "It's too hot. And The Keys don't even have good beaches, anyway." He paused. "I don't mean to make fun. I want to help. If it will help you do better work—"

"My work will be fine," said Moira. "There're stories to be told down there. You know that. It's the only way we'll get through to people."

"You're a a great reporter," said Martin. "But distractions certainly don't help."

"It's not a distraction," said Moira. "It's a motivator. Why do you think I pitched this project in the first place?"

"Fair enough," said Martin. "When's your flight?"

"Tomorrow," she had said, and here she was, piloting her tiny car down the Seven Mile Bridge, driving down from Miami to her bed-and-breakfast on Blackwell Key, the eastern-most of the Lower Keys, the first major landmass after the bridge. But Martin hadn't been wrong about her pride. She should have flown into Key West and drove up, instead of the other way around. Moira thought the drive would help ease her into the area. Let her understand the mindset. The Keys were a unique place, with a singular attitude, and she wanted to tap into that before she started talking to people. She already regretted the decision.

She'd only been on the long bridge for over a mile, and

she felt the tension rising inside her. Her chest had tightened, and her breath was coming harder, and she was trying to avoid looking to her right and left, the vast expanse of nothing but blue stretching out as far as she could see, the enormous abyss waiting to swallow her whole.

Moira tried to focus on the road, on the failing AC, but her peripheral vision picked up the stretch of unending blue. Her breath hitched, and her throat closed, and she felt it there, below her.

The darkness drew her down, grasping tar forming fingers and pulling her down, without breath, without life

She gasped, the car swerving, and she dragged it back straight. She was alone on her stretch of highway. Moira pulled off to the side, putting her flashers on.

Moira focused on her breath, just like she'd been taught, forcing her lungs open, her eyes closed. It was true, the water was there, and she could feel it, but she was safe, and she *could* breathe. A few more miles and she'd be there, at the Blue Dolphin Bed & Breakfast, with firm ground beneath her feet. She opened her eyes and looked out over the water.

The color shifted, from turquoise to deep blue, the depth and color of the sandy bottom playing with the colors, and Moira saw the beauty there, but it didn't stop the sea of anxiety that floated in her mind.

You have control.

She did have control, and she checked her mirrors and pulled back onto the highway. She breathed again. The deep fear that had seized her fell back into the recess it normally slept in.

Her worries subsided into surface level anxiety, of the

troubles she'd certainly have trying to pull together her piece, and of sleeping tonight after the mountain of caffeine she'd had during the day. She even appreciated the beauty of the mid-afternoon sun shining off the shallow water. Moira caught sight of a sunken key, and she noted it. She should mention it in her piece.

Then she saw the end of the Seven Mile Bridge, and a large sign welcoming her to Blackwell Key, a smiling cartoon grouper positioned on the right of it. US 1 cut right through the middle of it, the southern half mostly comprised of businesses and small hotels, the northern side all tiny lots of residents, mostly mobile homes. The key seemed small, but was still sizable compared to a lot of the others, minute blips and dots of lands between the bigger keys like Big Pine, Cudjoe, and of course, Key West.

She followed her GPS to the bed-and-breakfast, on the southern side of the island, right on the water. She parked in the sandlot and hauled her suitcase in, the wheels sinking into the dirt. The Blue Dolphin had only three suites, and in the off-season, Moira didn't expect any company there.

A bell rang as she entered the cramped office, and a short, older woman sat behind a counter, staring at her phone. She looked at it for a second longer and then put it down, standing up to speak to Moira. The room smelled like salt water, and all the decorations were either white shell or turquoise.

"Well, hello," said the woman, a large smile on her face. "You must be Ms. Bell."

"That's me," said Moira. The woman was still short, even standing up, with a small shock of dyed blond hair on her head. She was round and dressed in all white. As Moira approached the counter, the cutting scent of salt grew even stronger. She'd have to get used to it. It surrounded them.

"I'm Bea," she said. "We spoke on the phone. It's nice to meet you."

"Nice to meet you as well," said Moira.

"I've got a few pieces of paperwork for you, and then I can get you settled in," said Bea, grabbing the papers, scrawling on them quickly, and then handing them over to Moira.

"Sounds good," said Moira, looking it over quickly before signing. She handed them back.

Bea grabbed some keys from a shelf behind her and smiled. "Follow me."

The trip wasn't far. Bea led Moira to the largest of their three suites, all of which overlooked the ocean. The outside was painted purple.

"This is the Marlin," said Bea. "But I call it the purple palace. You can park underneath here." The suite was on stilts, like a lot of homes here, and below was room for storage and parking.

"How are you recovering from the hurricane?" asked Moira. The storm from three years past had destroyed a large part of the tourist industry here, and Moira was going to include some of it in her piece.

"Mostly alright," said Bea, as they climbed the steps. "Renovations are all done, so don't you worry about that. We're missing some trees here and there, but those will be the last things replaced. Sometimes I'm not sure if it's worth it at all, considering we're always in the line of fire, you know." Bea reached the top of the stairs and slid in the key, opening up the room to Moira's suite. "After you."

Moira walked in, and it wasn't only the outside that was purple. Everything inside was the same, with violet, lavender, and plum everything. It was full of beachy decorations, all various shades of purple.

"Oh. Wow," said Moira, walking into the living space. The kitchen was adjacent, with the bedroom in the front.

"So pretty, isn't it?" asked Bea.

"Oh, yes," said Moira, mustering up fake enthusiasm. "Beautiful."

"The bedroom is right through here," said Bea, leading Moira. Moira followed. The bedroom was roomy, with a king-size overstuffed mattress. A small dresser had a flat screen television on top. Two french doors opened up onto a narrow balcony, which overlooked the water. Bea opened up the doors. The sounds of waves crashing filled the room and the same feeling from on the bridge hit Moira again, just for a moment, jolting her, and then it was gone.

"You alright?" asked Bea.

"Yeah," said Moira, blinking away her feelings, turning her back on the ocean and putting her luggage on the bed.

"Bathroom's right here," said Bea. "I'll have breakfast ready for you downstairs anytime before ten. You just pop on down and I'll cook it up for you. Any other questions?"

"Not right now," said Moira. "I think I just want to rest for the moment. Been a long day of travel."

"I understand, I understand," said Bea. "You said you were a reporter? You down here for a story?"

"Yes."

"Can I ask what about?"

"Climate change," said Moira. "And how it will affect the people of coastal areas like the Keys."

A strange noise came from Bea, something between a sigh and a cough. "Nothing but a bunch of hogwash if you ask me."

"Can I ask where you get your news?"

"Mostly through Facebook."

"Do you mind if I interview you for my story sometime?"

"Well, no," said Bea, smiling again.

Moira turned away to write herself a note, and her eyes caught Bea in the mirror that sat in the corner of the bedroom. Bea's eyes were on Moira's back, and then something was off with her face, her round flesh softening and moving, pulling away from her cheekbones, and then Moira jolted back, to look at Bea straight on, and she was normal again. Moira blinked.

"You sure you're okay?" asked Bea.

"I've had too much caffeine," said Moira. "I need to just sit for a while."

"Amen to that," said Bea. She handed over the keys. "Call me if you need anything. I'm right downstairs."

Bea left Moira alone in the purple palace with the sound of waves. She slumped down on the bed, her eyes suddenly tired. What was that she saw in the mirror?

She pushed it away, her mind playing tricks on her. Too much stress today.

She looked at her phone. It was almost five o'clock. She knew she should go out and mingle, to absorb some of the ambiance from one of the island's late night spots, but she could barely find the energy to move. The sound of the water had seeped inside her.

She mustered the strength to push her luggage off the bed before she fell deep asleep, the crashing waves overwhelming her.

2

"How do you want your eggs?" asked Sally, the waitress.

"Over easy," said Moira.

She sat in a small booth in the half empty dining room of The Runny Egg Diner, the only 24-hour restaurant on Blackwell Key. If she was going to write a lifestyle piece on the island and its residents, she would need to get to know it. And as hackneyed as it was, diners were still a good place to do it.

She had passed on breakfast at the Blue Dolphin, drowning herself in coffee this morning as she did some preliminary brainstorming early. Moira slept through the night, the crashing waves hypnotizing her, but she woke with a headache. The caffeine bombardment had eased it, even if she could still sense it there, waiting behind her left eye. She swallowed the last of her mug. She'd put off the incoming pain as long as she could.

"Fill you up?" asked Sally.

"Please," said Moira.

"You're staying at the Blue Dolphin, right?"

"Yes," said Moira. "Word travels fast."

"It's a small place," said Sally. "Especially in the off-season. Heard you're a reporter?"

"I am."

"What's the story?" asked Sally. Moira eyed her. Sally was young, in her early 30s. It was worth a shot.

"Climate change," said Moira, watching Sally's face, looking for her reaction. Moira judged it as confusion. Could be worse. It could be rage.

"Isn't that like a hundred years away?" asked Sally.

"No," said Moira. "It's affecting us now, and places like Blackwell Key more than most."

"Oh," said Sally. "Your eggs should be right out." She wandered off to refill other coffees, and Moira considered that a better reaction than Bea's. She looked out the window, to the A1A, just outside. Cars and trucks passed by, none going fast. It seemed everything down here moved at a leisurely pace. There were no emergencies in Blackwell Key. She checked her phone, seeing that Joan Dermott still hadn't answered her text.

Sally delivered her eggs and toast, and Moira ate slowly. Maybe the food would help forestall her burgeoning headache. The eggs were good, cooked properly, and the rye bread hit the spot. She might skip Bea's breakfast every morning. Her phone buzzed on the table.

Hey, you're free to come by anytime. Sorry for the delay,

had a rough start

Moira replied, and finished the rest of her meal, paying and heading back to her car. Joan lived on the north side of the island. It was only a few minutes away, but Moira wasn't going straight there.

She had seen The Runny Egg, but if she was going to get a real idea of the island, she would need to see the whole thing at ground level. She had bought a map, and she pulled out of the parking lot, following her sketched out route.

Her waitress Sally was right. Blackwell Key wasn't big. Population in the off-season was under a thousand, but its size was a virtue. The smaller the place, the more vulnerable it would be, and Moira would use that vulnerability as an asset in her piece.

"We'll make them care," Martin had said. "Numbers mean nothing to people. Personal disasters do. You want to convince someone that climate change is real? Break their heart, and they'll believe."

The hurricane had hit Blackwell hard a few years back, and did so because of the changes wrought by climate change. Moira had done some research and found Joan Dermott, a local resident, fighting to stay one. Moira knew there was more story here, in a place so beautiful but so vulnerable. Bea didn't believe in climate change, but in twenty years her bed-and-breakfast wouldn't be accessible by road.

Moira drove down A1A, and then turned left, to the southern half of the island. She cruised past small cafes and condos, and the single hotel that operated on the island, its parking lot mostly empty. Most seemed to be operating as normal, even if you could still see signs of renovation and rebuilding on the edges. Landscaping still not quite fixed, or a few shingles missing, here or there. Moira noted anything unusual. She'd revisit those places. She would dig and see if she would find treasure.

But there wasn't much, not on the south side. Most businesses had bounced back. Or the ones that had failed had been papered over. She would have to do more research on that.

The north side told a different story. For every house that looked brand new with beautiful landscaping was a half destroyed mobile home or an empty lot, holes still in the ground from where the palm trees were torn up. Moira cruised up and down the streets, the ocean never more than a mile from her, no matter where she was on the island.

She slowed as she passed Blackwell Marina, also the home of Blackwell Sport Fishing, the biggest moneymaker on the island. The internet raved about their service, and the sport fishing community, as far as Moira could tell, considered Butch Blackwell one of the top fisherman on the planet.

His name wasn't a coincidence. His great, great, great grandfather had settled Blackwell Key. Butch was also the chief of police.

Butch could wait. She was almost done her tour, and she noted the still impacted homes on her map. She pulled up to Joan's house, and she immediately saw the damage.

A blue tarp had been pulled over the roof, held down by cinderblocks and rope. There was another pile of construction materials in the yard, also covered in a tarp.

There were no trees on the lot.

"You must be Moira," said a voice, and then Moira saw Joan, sitting on a lawn chair on a small wooden patio. Joan took a long drag from a cigarette and blew the smoke out in a blue-gray plume. Joan's blond hair was tied back in a sloppy ponytail, and her tired eyes were plain to see. But her shoulders were broad, and the muscles in her arms flexed as she moved.

"I am," said Moira, extending a hand. Joan took it, softly shaking it once, twice, and then letting go. "And you must be Joan."

"Guilty as charged," said Joan. "Welcome to Case de Dermott. Let me give you the dime tour. Seems only fair after you've come all this way." Joan stood up, still carrying her half-smoked cigarette, a thin trail of smoke leading behind her. Joan pushed through a screen door and Moira followed, doing her best to avoid the smoke. "I apologize for the mess. But there's not much use in cleaning."

Moira didn't understand at first, but then saw what Joan meant. There was an enormous hole in both the wall and the floor.

"Jesus," said Moira.

"Yeah, not ideal," said Joan, taking another puff. "Storm surge came right through here and flooded this half of the house. Debris put the hole in the wall and roof. Rot took the floor."

"And you had applied for relief from FEMA, correct?" asked Moira, pulling out her notepad.

"Yeah," said Joan. "But they haven't released me the money, and even if they did, there's not enough to make the repairs I need." Moira scribbled down notes.

"And you and your husband have lived like this for two years?" asked Moira.

"Yeah," said Joan. "We've made do. We've had to." Another puff. Moira could see her fingers tremble slightly as she fiddled with her cigarette. "You get used to it, after a while. We still have most of a roof, and luckily it never gets too hot or too cold down here."

"Mind if I take some pictures?" asked Moira.

"Feel free," said Joan. Moira used her phone to take pictures of all the damage.

"How long have you lived here?" asked Moira.

"Thirteen years," said Joan. "Grew up in Miami. Moved here for a job and met Bill. Chasing dreams, you know. Didn't quite work out."

"What do you both do for work?" asked Moira.

"We work for Butch," said Joan. "Hell, half the town works for him, in one way or the other."

"What do you do for him?"

"Hired hands on boats, mostly," said Joan. "Both of us know the water like the back of our hand. I grew up working on the water when I was young." Moira looked again at the muscles in Joan's forearms as she fiddled with her cigarette. "Mind if we go back to the patio?"

Moira snapped a couple more pictures. "Sure."

They went back out and Joan sat down where Moira had found her. Her smoke had nearly burned down, and she popped out another from the pack sitting on a small glass table, chaining it before snubbing out the old one.

"I don't like spending time in there, if I can help it," said Joan.

"I don't blame you," said Moira. "Were you here, when

it happened?"

"Yeah, we stayed," said Joan. "It was only a Cat 2, you know? Easy peasy. Living down here, you expect hurricanes, but most of the time they pass you by, with a little rain and some wind. Sure, if they get bad, you batten down the hatches and get the hell out of dodge, but mostly it doesn't happen. Maybe we've been lucky. But I swear it's been getting worse. We never used to get storm surge so bad."

"Do you think climate change has affected the weather?"

"I mean, yeah," said Joan. "You'd have to be blind to not see it. More storms. Bigger swings in temperature. I watch the news. It seems like there's more fires, more tornadoes. But no one here wants to hear it. They live in paradise. They don't want to think about it."

"The waitress at the Runny Yolk told me it'd take a hundred years," said Moira.

"A hundred years before we're completely underwater, maybe, but we have to drive around, you know, and even on the high side of the island we're only a foot above sea level."

"Does anyone talk about that here?"

"No," said Joan, shaking her head, with another long drag of her cigarette. "It's frustrating. The old timers, if you ever sit with them, they'll tell stories about how far you could walk out when they were kids. About walking to Little Mouse Key from the southern tip of Blackwell."

"I didn't see any Little Mouse Key in my research," said Moira.

"That's because it doesn't exist," said Joan. "It's underwater now. You can go snorkeling and see it, see where there used to be trees before they got swamped. But you tell 'em it's global warming and they stare at you like you got three heads."

"It's hard for some people to understand," said Moira. "With changes that happen so slowly."

Joan shook her head. "Fucking Butch. I tried to tell him to talk to the government down in Key West about it, but he won't do a thing. I know they're doing a few things in Miami, but they won't even entertain the idea of asking for money, asking for help. In ten, twenty years, some of these people are going to have to move. And they aren't ready. Just like I wasn't. And that's not even if a big storm sweeps through. There's one brewing out there now. Emile. Hope it misses us."

"You talk to Butch a lot?" asked Moira.

"Not a lot," said Joan. "Bill talks to him more. Or he did."

"He did? Not anymore?" asked Moira.

"Oh shit," said Joan. "Sorry. My brains have been scrambled lately, with so much going on. Bill's missing. Left in the middle of the night with our boat. Haven't heard from him."

"I'm—I'm sorry," said Moira. "I didn't realize."

"Don't apologize," said Joan. "I would say that I hope he comes back, but I don't think that's realistic."

"Do you know why he left?" asked Moira.

"No idea," said Joan. "I was over at a friend's for a get together. I came back and he was gone. The boat, too."

"Had he acted strangely at all, recently?"

"That's the thing, no," said Joan. "And I can read him

like a book. He was acting normal as all get out. And he didn't take anything. What little money we have is still in the bank, and he didn't pack any clothes. No notes, and he's not answering his phone."

"Did you inform the authorities?"

"I told Butch, but haven't heard anything. He just—just disappeared."

"When was this?" asked Moira.

"Six days ago," said Joan. "I keep expecting him to pull up in his truck. But he keeps not doing it."

"I really am sorry," said Moira. Moira studied Joan as she took another puff on her cigarette. "Will you be okay?"

"I'll have to be," said Joan. "No other choice. I keep thinking about Unsolved Mysteries, the old show. You remember that?"

"Yeah, when I was a kid," said Moira.

"They would find people with amnesia," said Joan. "Maybe that's what happened to Bill. Even if he ran off, I just—I just want to know he's okay."

"They might still find him," said Moira, but she could hear the doubt in her own words.

"You planning on talking to Butch for your story?" asked Joan.

"Yes," said Moira. "Tomorrow. He would only consent to the interview if I booked a trip out on his boat."

"That sounds like Butch," said Joan.

"I'm not looking forward to it," said Moira. "But I need to talk to him. The place is named after him."

"Don't worry about forgetting that," said Joan. "Butch sure as hell hasn't."

"Thank you for your time, Joan," said Moira. "It was

nice to meet you. If it's okay, I might follow up with additional questions while I'm here."

"That's fine," said Joan. "I'll do my best to help."

Moira got up to leave, leaving Joan in her lawn chair. Joan's voice stopped her.

"You watch yourself around Butch," said Joan, her voice cutting. Moira turned.

"What do you mean?" asked Moira. "Is he a creep?"

Joan stared at her, cigarette in hand. "No. Nothing like that. Just keep your guard up. He was the last person to talk to Bill."

3

"What do you think about that, Ms. Bell?" yelled Butch Blackwell over the choppy surf. "Isn't that a sight to see?"

Moira nodded at him, and forced a smile, but she didn't move from her spot in the center of the boat. She'd been on boats before, many times. Even after the panic attack on the bridge yesterday, she thought she'd be fine today.

She had been overconfident. Cold sweat clung to her, even under the hot Florida sun. Her knees, ankles, and feet ached, a sickly pain that was entirely nerves.

Butch stood on the edge of the boat, pointing down toward a shipwreck.

"It sank right after World War II," said Butch. "Got driven into shallow water by a storm and didn't see the reef. My daddy told me about all these navy men swimming back to the Key, waiting for pickup. Damndest thing. You sure you don't want to get a closer look?"

"I'm sure," said Moira. "I'm fighting off some sea-sickness."

"Oh hell," said Butch. "We got some nausea medicine. Bobby, get her some of the puke pills."

Butch was tall, standing over a foot taller than Moira, a thick head of blond hair covered by a trucker cap bearing the logo of Blackwell Sport Fishing. He was doughy, but the muscles in his shoulders and forearms stood out, much like Joan. She didn't doubt his strength. Moira pegged him in his mid-40s, but there was something in his face that made her question her guess. Something timeless, ageless.

A deckhand working in the back of the boat went below deck and returned a minute later with a couple of pills.

"These will do the trick, ma'am," he said, handing them over, and offering her a bottle of water.

"Thanks," she said, swallowing them wordlessly, doubting they would do anything at all. Nausea wasn't the problem here. It was the infinite, depthless void that reached out to her, threatening to pull her—

"That'll do you right up," said Butch, walking back toward her.

"Mr. Blackwell—"

"Please, call me Butch," he said, smiling, his face overtaken by it. The smile transformed him into something entirely different, and Moira didn't like it.

"Butch," said Moira. "Can I interview you now?"

"Well, sure, Ms. Bell," he said. "I ain't accustom to all of this, you know. Normally I just show people around and then we catch some fish."

"I understand," said Moira. Moira wore trunks and a long sleeve swim shirt, a wide brim hat on her head. She had bought the hat in a shop in town. She wanted to avoid the effects of the sun if at all possible.

"Well, shoot, then," said Butch. "Bobby, take us out to the normal spot." The boat cruised back up to speed. It was a large boat, over fifty feet, and Butch had three crewmen with him. They scurried about the boat around them, even if Moira didn't always know what they were doing.

"How has the hurricane affected the island? How has clean up gone?" asked Moira, pulling out a notepad from her small bag.

"Oh, it was rough at first," said Butch. "But it always is. Living down here, you're right on the edge of civilization. That's part of the charm! Out of reach. A little dangerous, even. But we been hit by storms as long we've been down here, and we pull ourselves back up by our bootstraps and rebuild. It's the nature of the beast."

"It's been two years since the last major hit, correct?" asked Moira.

"Just about," said Butch.

"And there's still residents who haven't rebuilt," said Moira. "People living out of houses with holes in the roof, with tarps covering half of their homes."

"I can't *make* people rebuild," said Butch. "It's a free country, y'know? But we got hit hard, just like everyone else. But we didn't sit around on our hands. We got back to work, patched up what we could, replaced what was left, and went back to business as usual."

The boat bounced off a big wave, and Butch whooped. Moira's breath caught in her chest.

"Man, I love it!" he yelled, pulling off his cap to ruffle his hair before replacing it.

"Are you worried at all about climate change?" asked Moira. "About the effect it will have on the island?"

"You believe that nonsense?" asked Butch.

"Yes," said Moira.

"Everything I've seen said that it's just the way the world is," said Butch. "Cycles. It's been hot before, and there ain't nothing we can do about it." Moira looked at Butch, trying to read him, but she couldn't see past his face. She'd met plenty of people who had used that same excuse to deflect discussion. And she was sure some of them believed it. But something in Butch's voice told her he knew better, that he was repeating talking points he'd heard on the news.

"The south side of Blackwell Key is how high above sea level?" asked Moira.

"About a foot," said Butch.

"On average," said Moira. "But I looked it up, and it said several spots are only a few inches. Including a few major access roads. Storm surge hasn't affected the island?"

"Of course it has, it always does during hurricanes—"

"I'm not talking about hurricanes," said Moira. "When it rains at all. You've had to have had flooding problems with any major rainfall."

"I mean, sure, sometimes," said Butch. "But everyone knows when it's going to rain, Ms. Bell. That ain't no problem."

Moira scribbled in her notes as the ocean spray bounced out from under the boat.

"You're also the Chief of Police on Blackwell Key?"

asked Moira.

"Guilty as charged," said Butch. "Not much of a job, really. Got three deputies, but we mostly just make sure people don't litter out on the water, and keep off of the private islands."

"Private islands?" asked Moira.

"Yeah," said Butch. "We got a few of them around us. Tiny little things, but they're privately owned, and you get tourists trying to set up shop to camp or picnic on 'em. Can't have that."

"Where are they?" asked Moira.

"Two are south of the Key," said Butch. "You're staying at the Blue Dolphin, right? You should be able to see one, Bear Key. The other, Stamp Key, is a little east of it. The third is north of Blackwell. Dagger Key."

"Who owns them?" asked Moira.

"Bear and Stamp Key are owned by private companies. Maybe they mean to develop them one day."

"And Dagger?"

"Oh, that's me," said Butch. "Been in the family for a long time."

"I didn't realize," said Moira. "I knew the Blackwells had settled the Key, but I didn't know you still had your own island."

"It's not that big," said Butch. "Just big enough for a little retreat for me and the missus, whenever we feel like disconnecting. Got a small homestead set up there, nice and sheltered like."

"Do you own any other land on the Key?" asked Moira.

"Just the marina and our home and the lot it sits on," said Butch. "The rest became public land long before I was born."

"Do you still feel like the Key is your responsibility? It carries your name, you're the Chief of Police, you have the largest business on the island."

"I mean, sure, I guess," said Butch. "I don't think about it too often. That was all well before my time, or my daddy, or my granddaddy. I'm just following in their footsteps. Trying to make the Key a good place for everybody."

He smiled again, that same disconcerting smile, and it clicked into place. He was performing for her. None of these answers were Butch, and she hadn't seen the real Butch yet at all.

"We're out, Butch," said Bobby, behind the wheel.

"Beautiful day for it, too," said Butch, the enormous smile still on his face, even as he spoke through it. "You sure you don't want to catch anything? It's grouper season."

"I'm good," said Moira.

"Are you a vegetarian?" asked Butch.

"No," said Moira. "Not a big fan of the water."

"Oh, don't worry about that," said Butch. "The fish is the one in the water. You're safe up here on the boat."

"I really don't—"

"Oh, come on, Ms. Bell," said Butch. "I can help you with your story. A little fishing never hurt nobody."

More performance. Moira's stomach ached and her chest tightened, but she stood up, and followed Butch's smile to the back of the boat, where rows of fishing poles were lined up. She'd never seen rigs like this, thick, with a heavy line.

"I got this one set up, just for you," he said.

"The line's already in the water," said Moira.

"That's how sport fishing works," said Butch. "We trail live bait behind the boat, with long lines, to catch the big fish. Grouper, blue marlin."

"Oh," said Moira. She traced the lines into the dark water. "How deep is it here?"

"It varies, but at least over 250 feet," said Butch. "That's where you'll usually find the huge ones. Deeper the better."

At hearing the depth, the backs of her knees tightened, and her breath halted again. She swallowed and took a deep breath through her nose. *You can handle it, Moira.*

"You alright, Ms. Bell?" he asked. "If you're gonna throw up, I'd ask that you try and do it overboard."

"No—"

And then one of the reels suddenly jolted, the line spinning out. Billy's voice called out. "Fish on!"

"Oh hell," said Butch. "It's your time, Ms. Bell. I can already tell this is a big boy. You gonna be able to handle it?"

Moira looked to Butch, and realized this was her ticket to respect on Blackwell Key. She swallowed the anxiety and nodded.

"Atta girl! Here, sit right here, this is your throne," he said, and grabbed the fishing pole in one smooth action, reeling it with hard, quick movement as he carried it to her. "Now reel, reel, reel. You want that pole bending."

Moira grabbed it and cranked, the big reel spinning as she pulled in foot after foot of line out of the opaque water. The anxiety and worry were all gone. Her arm burned as she spun and spun. Her cardio was good, but she didn't have the strength training for this.

"Keep going, even if you slow down," said Butch. "You

let up on the tension, the fish will shake the hook loose."

The minutes crawled by, and she cranked on the reel, the muscles in her arm burning, but she didn't let up. She would catch this damn fish, even if it took all day.

But as she reeled, the anxiety returned. The awful anxious pain that dwelled in her joints, in her stomach, in her lungs and chest. Of the feeling of the deep, coming up to pull her under. To subsume her. That whatever was on the other end of that hook wasn't some game fish. It was something else.

But she couldn't stop reeling. Her arm had become part of the fishing pole now, one with the reel. She was all machine, all a tool to bring it up from the deep, and she couldn't stop, even as all of her burned with pain and fear and horror.

"Reel, reel, reel!" yelled Butch, and she could see the same smile, the massive grin that ate up his face, and she reeled, she couldn't not reel, she had to bring it up, pull that horror to the surface.

It was infinite and sudden and the horror was there, and Butch brought it in next to the boat, and it was just a fish.

"Come look at it," he said, and Moira could move again, her reeling done. It was a blue marlin, massive. "You're a natural, I tell you."

The crew surrounded her, all of them taking in the marlin. "Catch and release," said Butch, and she nodded, and then he cut it loose, the fish swimming down below. Moira realized herself then, and she was right next to the edge, and she handed the pole to Butch and retreated to the middle of the boat, where she had started, all the adrenaline flowing out of her. She glanced at the clock and realized that forty-five minutes had passed.

Moira looked back, quickly, at all the men on the boat, all bunched up, and they blurred in her vision, their faces a mess of something she couldn't recognize, a dark obscure blotch.

But then it was gone, and she was alone with her anxiety again, stronger now. She focused on her breathing. There was no pulling over here, only being on the boat or not.

"Congrats, girl!" yelled Butch. "You ready to head back?"

"Yes," said Moira, forcing the word out. "I lost track of time, there."

"It happens," said Butch. "You sit in that chair, with the pole in your hand, and reality shifts. It's crazy. I love it!" and he whooped loudly, taking off his hat again, and she still saw only performance. But the boat turned again, and they headed back to Blackwell Key.

She remembered Joan's words about Butch. About watching him.

He sat across from her, staring out over the water, in a trance.

"What do you think happened to Bill Dermott?" asked Moira, suddenly, and Butch's face changed, emptying. She watched him, like Joan had told her to. And for the first time, Butch dropped his performance, if only for a moment. He hadn't expected to hear that name.

"What do you mean?" asked Butch, his face re-shifting, collecting itself again. Reconstructing its facade in just a moment.

"He's missing, isn't he?" asked Moira. "Took his boat and left?"

"Have you been talking to Joan?" asked Butch.

"Just curious about your take on it. You are the police, and he worked for you, right?" asked Moira.

"My take?" asked Butch. That moment of truth had passed. Performance again. "My take is that Bill wanted a break from Joan, but he didn't see a way out except running in the middle of the night. We've kept an eye out for his boat. Let the Sheriff know. But nothing. He just vanished. Maybe he'll come back. You never know."

Moira paused, but Butch volunteered nothing else. They were drawing closer back to the Key, and Moira felt the tension in her chest ease, just a little.

"That's Dagger Key, right there," said Butch, pointing to a island as they passed. Blackwell Key was within sight.

"It's pretty close," said Moira.

"Just close enough, is what my daddy always said," said Butch. Moira looked, but couldn't see anything but tree cover.

"Looks like a lot of trees," said Moira.

"Helps keep people off," said Butch. "Gives us some cover, too. Easier than putting up walls."

But then the boat was pulling back into the marina, its speed low, and Moira found her breath full again, her throat open. She hadn't realized how much trouble she'd had until she stepped back onto the dock, and then finally on land again. It was mid-afternoon, and the sun still shone, but it felt like she had been out on the boat for days.

"That was quite a catch out there, Ms. Bell!" whooped Butch. His face was a mask again, smiling widely. "Has anyone invited you to the potluck yet?"

"I guess not," said Moira.

"Well, let me be the first," said Butch. "It's at the community center. Don't worry about bringing anything, there'll be plenty of food. But if you want to talk to people, there's your chance. See you there?"

"Sounds good," said Moira. Butch smiled even wider, and Moira felt her stomach tighten, and then he was gone, and she could breathe again.

She remembered Joan's words. Keep an eye on him.

She understood them now.

4

The long table at the back of the main hall of the community center was stuffed with casseroles. Every type of casserole that Moira had ever eaten, along with many others she'd never seen before. Most of them were seafood based, with shrimp, crab, and all kinds of fish, baked with pasta, with rice, in pie crusts.

"Make sure you try one of everything, dearie," said a kindly old lady at her elbow, who reached past her to get some of a craberole. "Got to get a taste of it all." She leaned in closer. "And that way you won't hurt nobody's feelings." The elderly woman cackled, a big steaming pile of food on her paper plate. "Bea tells me you're a reporter."

"That's right. I'm Moira," she said. "I'd offer a hand—"

"Oh, don't worry about that, sweetheart," she said. "I'm

Sarah. It was so nice to invite you to our little get together. We get new people so rarely. Would you like me to introduce you around?"

"That'd be great," said Moira. Sarah was a short, rotund old lady, probably in her 70s, shorter even than Moira herself. She wore a church dress that looked like it came from 1983. Seeing how old Sarah was, it probably was.

"Then you better fill your plate honey," said Sarah. "And tell everyone that their casserole is delicious." She said it all with a smile. Moira scooped a little of every dish onto her plate, until it was overfull, much like the community center itself.

The tiny building was filled with people, bringing the room temperature up a few degrees, even with the AC blasting and the two overhead fans circulating. The building looked to be at least 30 years old, with the same wood paneling and beige carpet that Moira had seen all over the country in buildings just like this. The cheapest of the cheap. Butch held court at a corner table, with a loose assemblage of men in Columbia shirts and baseball caps listening to him, laughing uproariously once in a while at his loud jokes. Moira's eyes glanced over him, studying him as she followed Sarah. All performance.

Moira scanned over the rest of the people. She spotted Bea at another table. She looked for Joan in the crowd, either grabbing food, a drink, or sitting at a table, but nothing.

"You can sit here, honey," said Sarah, and Moira sat down next to Sarah at a round table filled with older women. They ranged in age, from their 40s to their 80s, and Sarah introduced them all to Moira. Moira did her best to remember all their names and faces. She typically did well with it, but she was sure she lost some along the way. They all smiled and bombarded Moira with questions, barely giving her time to respond before talking some more, every question and answer setting off a cascade of responses from around the table, leading them far astray from the starting point.

"What do you report on?" asked Marcia.

"Climate change," said Moira.

"Oh my," said Marcia. "For who?"

"Public radio," said Moira.

"I listen to that in the morning," said Marilyn. "I love the classical music."

"I've heard that's just more of that fake news," said Martha.

"You say that about everything," said Sarah.

And around they went. Moira smiled, and made mental notes, taking small bites of each casserole, doing her best to keep names and faces straight.

"Do you like my smoked salmon bake?" asked Marilyn.

"Oh yes," said Moira. "Very good."

"That's nice to hear," said Marilyn. "Hard to get real answers from anyone you've known for so long." The table talked in a whirl, and the community center got louder as time went on, as more and more people packed inside. Moira didn't think it was possible, and yet more people came in. The room was buzzing, and Moira still heard Butch in the corner, his voice carrying over the din.

Trying to steer the conversation with this many people was impossible, so she just absorbed their chatter, getting an idea of what living in Blackwell Key was like. And from the babble, it seemed like if you lived on Blackwell Key, there was nothing else.

Sure, there were trips to the grocery store on Big Pine, or to restaurants on nearby Keys, but the talk all centered on happenings on their island. On Blackwell.

Maybe it was just the group setting, but no one talked about anything too upsetting or too dangerous. No one brought up politics, and if they did, someone quickly changed the subject. Moira tried to focus on individuals, but the room was a blur, the cacophony surrounding her, overwhelming her. Her cheeks grew hot. She needed something cold.

"Pardon me, Sarah," she said. "I need a drink."

"Oh, no worries, dear," said Sarah, and Moira left, dodging past groups of people chatting.

"—Fish were biting like crazy—"

"—hear that storm is coming through—"

"—He'll be here soon—"

And then she was at the drinks table, with two big punch bowls set up. One was red and the other was purple. Moira opted for the red. There were ice cubes floating in it, and she just wanted something cold. She scooped some punch into a plastic cup and then turned directly into someone, the drink flying all over them.

"Oh god, I'm so sorry," she said. The red punch covered his white and blue striped button-up.

"It's okay," he said. "I was coming to get some, anyway." Moira grabbed some napkins from the table and helped wipe away the excess liquid.

"I should have watched where I was going," she said.

"It's perfectly alright," he said. "I have more shirts, and it's packed in here." He was taller than average, a slim build, but fit. His chestnut brown hair was cut short and parted to one side. He wiped off the rest of the excess punch and then studied her for a second. "You must be the reporter." He extended a hand. "I'm Mike."

"I am," she said, shaking his hand, still slightly sticky. "I'm Moira. Can I get you some punch? To drink, this time."

"That'd be great," he said. Moira filled two cups, handing one to him.

"Here, there's some space in the corner," he said, and she followed him, a little bit of breathing room in the cramped community center.

"Is it always this crowded?"

"Not always," said Mike. "But often. It's the peak of the off-season."

"Isn't that a contradiction?"

"Not really," he said. "Once you live here long enough, you recognize the patterns. Of people coming and going. Of the tourists visiting and then leaving."

"How long have you lived here?".

"Four years now," he said.

"What do you do?"

"I'm a police officer," said Mike.

"You work for Butch?"

"Yes," he said. "I did odd jobs around the island for a few years, handyman type stuff, and then he hired me on last year. Is this for your story?" He smiled.

"Yes and no," said Moira. "It's good to have background information. It colors everything."

"Can't argue with that," said Mike. "Butch told me you're here about climate change. About how our little island is going to be swallowed up by the sea." He took a long sip. Moira detected no sarcasm or irony in his voice.

"Yes," she said, smiling. "Basically."

"Having much luck?" asked Mike.

"Some, so far," said Moira. "People are talking to me, at least."

"Do people not talk to you?" asked Mike. "You seem nice enough to me."

"Some just turn off when I say the words climate change," said Moira. "They look at me like I have three eyes."

"Everyone here is polite," said Mike. "At least to your face."

"That's nice to know," said Moira. She sipped on her punch. Still no sign of Joan. Safe to say, she wouldn't be making an appearance.

"Well, are you going to ask me?" asked Mike.

"Ask you what?"

"If I believe in climate change."

"I don't like that question."

"Why not?" asked Mike.

"Because it makes it sound like it's religion," said Moira. "It's science. It's facts."

"Then what question do you ask?"

"Are you *prepared* for climate change?"

"That *is* a better question."

"Well?"

"Me?" asked Mike. "Hell no. I have a boat, but that doesn't mean much when I don't have anywhere to anchor it."

"That seems like the typical answer around here," said Moira.

"You're not wrong," said Mike. "I'm betting Butch didn't appreciate your questions."

"He mostly avoided them," said Moira. "Got me fishing instead."

"He mentioned you caught a nice marlin," said Mike.

"I did."

"You don't seem too happy about it."

"I'm not a big fan of the water."

"You must love it here, then," said Mike. "Why Blackwell?"

"Because it's at the front lines," said Moira. "You're one of the places that will see the effects first. You're already seeing them. Extreme storm surge and flooding, erosion. We want to make people aware of the danger coming, and soft news stories are maybe the thing. Not stories about inches of ocean rising, but people, suffering. And how worse it will get for them."

"You're trying to scare people?" asked Mike.

"I mean, yes," said Moira. "If that's what it takes." She glanced around again.

"Who are you looking for?"

"Joan Dermott."

"You won't find her here."

"Why not?" asked Moira.

"She's on the outs with Butch," said Mike. "I didn't tell you this, but they'd been icy toward each other even before Bill flew the coop, and now? Nothing." Moira glanced at Butch, who still stood in the corner. Butch's eyes flittered toward her and Mike and she cut her gaze away, quickly.

"What do you think happened with Bill?" asked Moira.

"Oh, I don't know," said Mike. "I knew him well enough, and he didn't seem like the type to cut and run. But that doesn't mean he didn't do it. Or maybe he just wanted some space to think. They've been having a tough time, and maybe after some time alone he'll come back with hat in hand. But Butch didn't handle Joan as delicately as I would have."

"What did he do?" asked Moira. "He told me he followed the proper protocols."

"He did what he was legally required to do," said Mike. "But not more than that. I'm pretty sure he assumes we'll never see Bill again. He's never liked Joan, even when she worked for him. Butch likes people who follow, and don't question him."

"And you're okay with that?" asked Moira.

"This is just a job," said Mike. "Not a career, if you understand that."

"I do," said Moira. "Anyone else around here I should talk to?"

"There's a couple hundred people in here," said Mike. "Don't want to talk to them?"

"Joan's not here," said Moira. "Who else isn't here?"

Mike stared at her for a second, a thoughtful look on his face. "Well, there's Houseboat. He'd be an interview, and there's no way in hell he'd ever show his face at one of these things."

"Houseboat?" asked Moira. "His name is Houseboat?"

"No, but that's what everyone calls him," said Mike. "I don't know his Christian name, to tell you the truth."

"What's his number?"

"I don't think he's got a phone," said Mike. "But this part of the year you can find him down at Seagull's."

"Seagull's?"

"It's a waterside bar," said Mike. "They got some docks, and they rent one out to him in the off-season, to make a little extra cash. No one'd use it otherwise."

"And I should talk to him?" asked Moira.

"He's very smart," said Mike. "And he's been here a long time. Don't be fooled by his appearance. He knows more than—"

"I see you found one of my deputies!" yelled Butch, stepping up to them, looming over them. "Hope you're not giving away all my secrets!"

"You don't have any secrets, Butch," said Mike. "Except maybe how you keep getting them damn fish to bite."

"That's all skill, son," said Butch. He smiled that same unsettling grin. "How you doing, Moira? Liking the potluck? I saw Sarah showing you around."

"Yes, she took care of me," said Moira. Something turned in her stomach, a twinge of pain and nausea, and her hand went to her torso reflexively.

"You okay?" asked Mike.

"Yeah, I'm—" said Moira, but then the pain ripped through her again, worse now, pulling a painful moan from her.

"Can I help?" asked Mike. Moira's eyes went to him, and then to Butch, the same awful smile on Butch's face, and then the pain and nausea doubled, and then doubled again.

"I can't—" and she was going to throw up. Where was

What Dwells Beneath The Waves

the bathroom, she didn't know, she pushed through the crowds of people, out the front door, into the cool night air. She found the bushes and threw up, all the tastes of strange casseroles pouring out of her mouth, splashing onto the ground, mixed with the fruit punch.

It was awful. The nausea was gone, but the pain still ripped through her guts. She wiped her mouth with the back of her hand and opened her eyes.

Moira glanced at what remained of her dinner on the ground, and almost looked away, but then she caught it moving, and she stared again.

Small fish flopped on the ground, covered in bile, their gills flexing as they gasped for breath, and it was too much, and she threw up again, and she could feel the creatures force their way out of her, the rough scales and fins rubbing on the inside of her throat and mouth. They came out in a torrent, and she coughed, forcing it all out. All she could taste was saltwater, toxic burning salt scorching her throat and nose.

She looked again, because she couldn't not, and it was just food, nothing but the remnants of some casseroles. She took a deep breath. What was happening to her?

Get a hold of yourself, Moira.

She'd had a long day, out on the water, in the sun. It was probably just heat stroke. She needed rest. The bed-and-breakfast was only a quarter mile away and they'd understand if she didn't say goodbye.

Moira turned to the B&B, her feet echoing off the sidewalk. The roar of the ocean rang through her ears.

The visions started halfway back.

5

They stood around the obelisk, and they awakened it with ocean water mixed with blood.

The water had to be warm, as warm as the blood, the salt bled into the wound, and then pushed into the obelisk, born out of a salted stone that did not exist but still was present. The salt burned the wound, but the pain was integral to the ritual. The suffering was necessary.

The wind howled, and the ocean roared a deep ambient din, surrounding them, as they each, one by one, pushed the salt into the deep wounds, the water swirling with blood, the basin filled with the briny claret, and the obelisk fed.

The obelisk fed, and the dark shadow that lurked in the burning water sent an emissary, sent a creature, a dark thing sliding out of the depths, onto shore.

Moira stumbled then, and she tried to focus on her steps, but she couldn't see, she saw nothing but the obelisk and the thing that dwelled beneath the waves and the blood brine that paid service to it. Her stomach burned, and she threw up again as she walked, but nothing but bile this time. She still walked, catching half sight of the sidewalk. She needed to get back to her bed; she was sick, and she needed sleep.

But the waves of visions didn't stop, and now she saw not *where* she was, but *when*, a sky and ground unrecognizable, an Earth she didn't know. The sky roiled in black, clouds of red and gray, burning through the air, prehistoric and raw. The ground hardened, with plants long dead and forgotten. But something walked on the surface, something impossible. More emissaries, more travelers, missionaries from below the waves, sent from a dark and large unknowable thing, creatures summoned from a darkened plane only accessible with a blackened mind. They stumbled out onto the burnt ground, breathing air for the first time, sloughing off toxic black sludge as they moved. The poison killed the small lichens as they walked, primitive life forms scrambling from underfoot.

The things trudged across the alien landscape, their softened features unrecognizable, blurred around the edges, something aquatic, amphibian, but those words were lies, because this came before, before anything but the most basic of life, and they tramped on dry land, always yearning for the water, spreading briny sludge wherever they went.

Moira stepped, the ocean roar loud in her ears, all that

she heard, the grasping sound of the sea reaching for as much land as it could before settling back, falling back. Her feet left the sidewalk, as she walked only half seeing, her mind's eye filled with things she couldn't know, and she was in the parking lot of The Blue Dolphin, and she tried to find the stairs to her suite, where she could collapse, and let this end, let her body rest even as she was assaulted.

But she couldn't locate them, her feet stomping onto the sand, and then into the water, the warm water, her toes sinking into the brown algae that painted the sea floor. Waves lapped at her ankles, and she tried to resist, no, no, not the water, but her legs carried her farther, until it was up to her knees.

The water was cold.

The water was cold, and Moira swam out, the hot Florida sun beating down on her. Her grandma lived in Vero Beach and they were visiting, and Moira was young, very young, and so, so small.

She ran in the sand, and her parents lazily watched, each reading a worn-down paperback, each in turn keeping an eye on Moira, but she was a font of limitless energy, and they let her play in the sand, and then she sprinted for the water, screaming that she was swimming, and they yelled after her, *don't swim too deep.*

She heard them but she didn't, like many words they said, entering her ears but not her mind, but it wouldn't have mattered, because she didn't want to go deep, she only wanted to play in the shallows.

They were the only occupants of that stretch of beach, still too early for the tourists to arrive and set up shop, but not too early that the sun already beat down, the sand warming up. The Atlantic water was cold, cold year round.

Moira skipped through the shallow water, her feet sinking into the wet sand, pulling her feet out gently with each step. The cold water felt nice on her feet, without a fear, without a worry. Only joy. The pure, unbridled joy of play.

She ventured deeper, ankle deep, and then up to her knees. She was tiny, and it wasn't very far. If she looked behind her she saw her parents, and she waved at them, and her mom waved back from underneath their beach umbrella.

Moira then looked back to the ocean, to the horizon, out to the water.

And then that's all there was, the immense ocean, an infinite plane of deep, dark blue. No beach, no land, only water. A well to fill the world, drawn from the deeps, from a depth that couldn't be measured.

Moira tried to pull back from the water.

She existed in both places, and she wanted to lie down, to sleep off whatever hell she was in, she was sick, but the dark night water pulled at her, a magnetic pull that she couldn't resist. The gentle waves crashed against her shins, and then her knees, and then her thighs, but she kept going out, and she knew it got deep suddenly, and she couldn't stop herself

She couldn't stop herself and she waded deeper into the cold, cold water, until the waves crashed against her chest, harder than she expected. But the deep water pulled at her, and she didn't know why, she just knew that she had to keep going. Soon she was neck deep, the cold water enveloping her, and if her parents looked out then, they would see only the tiny shock of dark hair poking out of the water, waves obscuring the view of their daughter, but neither looked, both nose deep in their books, the sounds of the crashing waves hypnotizing them.

The warm water welcomed her and Moira continued walking, the water over her waist now, her clothes soaked, and she still saw everything, all at once, her mind full of visions of the obelisk, of the primordial landscape, of the ritual and blood and of her own youth, and she tried to push it all out, because she only wanted to be back on shore, out of this depthless death but she couldn't, and pulled in anxious breath after breath, trying to jolt her body back into submission, but the deep called to her and she continued out and then the ground dropped off and she was beneath the water.

The cold welcomed her as she fell below the waves, the hot sun unable to penetrate the surface of the water, and it was dark down there, and cold, and it was then that she knew she would die here, that the dark infinite well had pulled her out here to kill her, to take her body forever into its own, and to never let her go. She felt the hands rising out of the inky darkness, formed and formless, grasping at her small ankles and shins, pulling her down beneath the crashing waves. Her parents had looked by now, and realized she had disappeared into the water, her father screaming for help and then sprinting into the waves.

Moira tried to breathe but only breathed in death the water, it was only water now, and she tried to push her way out of this womb, dark and formless and every direction was darkness, gravity disturbed, and she had ventured too far, they would find her dead on the shore in the morning, the reporter had vanished from the community potluck and had drowned; the words whispered by the townsfolk. The encompassing smile of Butch, and the empty, tired eyes of Joan Dermott, as she smoked a cigarette, waiting for her husband to return, hoping there was an escape.

Moira found feeling with her feet again, and they listened to her commands, and she kicked, pushing to the surface, but the water rose, higher and higher, warming, there is no surface anymore, there is only the water, only water.

Moira kicked, pushed to the surface, through cold and warm water, trying to escape its grasp, but inky hands of eldritch darkness pulled her down, grasped her ankles and dragged her and she needed air, please, but there was only water and she drowned.

Drowned, her heart slowed and then stopped, only water in her lungs. The water was home now, in the darkness. Death did not stop her from feeling the expanse, the infinite plane.

But she wasn't alone.

The inky hands, the toxic darkness that pulled her there and kept her there were gone, but there was something else, something she only sensed, sensed alongside everything else, and as she looked for it, she reached out for it. She *needed to know*

And then her father pulled her to the surface, his arms around her, pulling her out of the cold, cold water, carrying her to the sands, and a lifeguard was there, and she awoke with his hands on her chest, water pouring out of her lungs, her chest roaring with pain, but she breathed air again.

Her parents cried and held her, squeezing her tight.

Moira was on the sand again, bent over, vomiting dark bile out of her stomach, her clothes dry, in the darkness of the Keys.

Her throat and sinuses burned, and she spit up every ounce she had in her stomach. The memory of full lungs still hung in her, and her chest ached, and she pounded on it with a clenched fist, but she breathed air. She felt drunk, but she'd had nothing to drink, and her stomach was empty. Her palms rubbed against her shirt and jeans, and they were dry, the thought of walking into the ocean forgotten, imagined.

Not imagined. She had done it, as a child, and those memories blurred in her mind, along with visions. Visions of—

Visions of what, exactly?

An obelisk. And dark things, silhouetted against a primitive sky.

The images flashed through her mind, intermixed with all her trauma, and the pain in her chest and throat and gut, and no thoughts could form. She shook her head, and blinked hard, trying to force organization, but nothing happened, and she blearily saw the stairs up to her suite, and she reached for them, and her feet followed, and she climbed.

She staggered inside and pulled off her shoes before collapsing into bed. A tremendous exhaustion had swept through her, and she couldn't move, her eyes closing and her body falling into immediate, deep sleep.

A single vision danced behind her eyelids as her mind

collapsed.

An image of something down in the deep, below the waves, the other denizen she had reached for.

She had reached for it as a child, and she had reached for it tonight.

It slept, frozen. Deep, deep down.

And then it stirred.

6

It was past noon when Moira finally awoke, her body stiff and sore, her chest and throat aching. A root of pain had burrowed behind her right eye. She crawled out of bed, downing multiple glasses of water and a handful of ibuprofen.

The night before was a blur. She remembered feeling ill at the potluck, and then stumbling home. She had felt terrible, overwhelmed by dark memories. Her drowning. She had been lost inside it. She had gone into the water here, but she'd been dry. One of the casseroles must have been bad. She wondered if anyone else had gotten sick.

She'd left without saying goodbye to anyone. What was the deputy's name?

Mike. He'd been nice, and was worth following up on.

He had mentioned someone else. She sorted through the disparate thoughts of the night before.

What was the name? Something strange.

Houseboat.

At the docks at Seagull's. She didn't know the bar, but she'd find it. If she wanted to know Blackwell Key, she needed to talk to people outside of Butch's circle of influence.

After a few minutes the various aches and pains dulled because of the painkiller, and she took a hot shower, washing off the salt that had stuck to her skin—

You didn't go in the water

She dressed and looked up information on Seagull's. It wasn't far, a tiny dive bar on the shore. She drove and was there in under five minutes.

Seagull's was closed, the lights out, but she walked past it, down its dock, and saw the houseboat, gently rocking in the water, ropes straining, back and forth. *Darling* was painted on its stern.

Moira approached the boat slowly, the early afternoon sun beating down. A skinny, shaggy looking dude passed her, wearing a dirty tank top and ragged jeans. He smelled like smoke and BO.

What the hell?

"Hello?" she asked, knocking on the side of the boat.

She heard footsteps, suddenly, and some shuffling from inside, and then a man emerged, bare chested, his long silver hair tied back in a ponytail, dark sunglasses covering his eyes, and a bandanna fastened around his neck. He wore ratty khaki shorts and two worn flip-flops clung to his feet.

"Be careful, there, young lady," he said. "You'll knock down my house. Darling can only take so much." He stared at her for a second longer, and then smiled, taking off his sunglasses and perching them on top of his head. Moira didn't doubt the genuineness with him. "Just a joke. I'm Houseboat, pleased to make your acquaintance." He extended a hand, and Moira met it.

"Moira Bell," she said. "Nice to meet you."

"Like the telephone?" asked Houseboat.

"I guess," said Moira. "But it hasn't been Bell for a long time."

"Tells you my age," he said. "Can't stand the things, anyway. What can I do you for?"

"I'm a reporter," she said. "Here to talk to people about climate change."

"I knew it," he said. "I caught wind of somebody staying at the Blue Dolphin, asking questions. That must be you."

"Guilty as charged," said Moira.

"No shame in asking questions," said Houseboat.

"Do you have time for an interview?"

"I was just doing some building," said Houseboat. "But that can wait. I got all the time in the world. Or least all the time *left* in the world. Come aboard, I'll give you the dime tour."

Houseboat opened a small door, and extended a hand again, pulling Moira aboard. Anxiety bloomed in Moira's stomach, but she stayed in control.

"You alright?" asked Houseboat.

"Yeah, I'm fine. Not a big fan of water," she said.

"Neither am I, to be honest. I'm a shit swimmer," he

said. "I try and stay out of it."

"You're a shit swimmer, but you live in the Keys?"

"It's the most beautiful place on Earth," he said, leading her into the house part of the boat. The living room/kitchen was first, with a short couch to one side and a kitchenette on the other. It was larger on the inside. It felt like a home, if only a small one.

"This is my lounge and kitchen," he said. "Has everything I need. Gas-powered." A small desk stood to one side, with a miniature desk lamp and a tray filled with intricate model parts.

"What are you building?"

"A ship in a bottle."

"The rocking doesn't bother you?"

"You get used to it after a while," he said. "You anticipate the movement and adjust. Back there is my bedroom, and the bathroom is right here, in case you need it. Would you like a drink?"

"A water would be great," she said. "A soda even better."

"I've got Diet Coke, if that's okay."

"That's perfect," she said, and Houseboat grabbed one for her from the fridge.

"Sit anywhere," he said. Moira sat on a small folding chair, propped against the wall. Houseboat sat at his desk, in the lightweight office chair, the wheels popped off.

Moira took out her phone and set it down. "Do you mind if I record this?"

Houseboat eyed the phone and rolled his eyes. "You have one, man, so it's already recording us. Might as well have it on the record."

Oh god.

"I appreciate it," she said. "Does everyone call you Houseboat?"

"Almost everyone," he said.

"You mind telling me your given name?"

Houseboat eyed her and grinned. "I suppose. Hal McNally. But please call me Houseboat. I haven't gone by Hal in a long time."

"I'll do my best," said Moira. "How long have you lived here?"

"Here? Blackwell?"

"Sure."

"A few months," he said, smiling, and then waved her off. "I mostly live here during the slow season."

"Where do you go during the tourist season?"

"Oh, I flit around," he said. "Usually Key West, but I like to be mobile. To answer your question, I've been in the Keys for about twenty years, and most of that time has been spent here."

"Wow, that's a long time," said Moira. "Where were you before that?"

"San Francisco," he said. "In my past life."

"What was it like?"

"My past life?" he asked. "Different. Busy. I saw a chance to get out, and I took it. I don't regret it. Life down here suits me better."

"How would you describe life here?" asked Moira.

"Measured," said Houseboat, after a brief pause. "Not to say people don't move fast at times, but it feels nice and slow."

"Does that ever feel like a double-edged sword?"

"What do you mean?"

"I'll ask a different question," said Moira. "Do you think Blackwell and its people are ready for climate change?"

Houseboat laughed, a big, heavy laugh out of his chest. He laughed for a few more seconds. "No, of course not. Most think its a boogeyman made up by overreactive scientists."

"The effects can already be seen here," said Moira. "Have you noticed any changes over your time here?"

"Sure, I have. A few tiny islands, here and there, have less and less land above the water. Couple have been wiped out altogether by the hurricanes. There's a little less beach, here and there."

"Do you ever worry about it?" asked Moira.

"Of course I do," said Houseboat. "I think most rational people do. But it won't affect me. I'll be long dead before it gets bad. Lousy to say, but I think that's how a lot of people rationalize their behavior."

"Do you think there's anything people could do to help?"

Houseboat looked at her for a second, thinking.

"I think acknowledging a problem is the first step," he said. "But that's not going to happen."

"Mike told me you don't have a phone."

"I don't," said Houseboat. "Anyone that needs me knows where to find me. What else did Mike say about me?"

"I was at the potluck last night, and Joan Dermott wasn't there."

"Of course not," he said. "Not while Butch is there."

"And I asked if I could talk to someone else who wouldn't attend them, and he suggested you."

"That's not a bad suggestion," he said. "'Cause it's true. I'd never go to one of those things."

"Why not?"

Houseboat sighed. "Don't get along with Butch myself, to be honest. Never been much for law and order, even in my last life. Don't see much the need for police, especially in a place like this, where all he does is cruise around on his boat and tell people where they belong."

"Some might say him being chief of police is a conflict of interest," said Moira.

"They wouldn't be wrong," said Houseboat. "But he's just more flagrant than others. When the place is named after you, and you've got your own private island right offshore, it makes it more obvious. But the police is only there to protect property, not people. Everybody likes Butch, so he continues to be the chief."

"But you don't?" asked Moira.

Houseboat eyed her phone, the number slowly ticking up as it recorded them. "Is all of this going in your piece?"

"No, probably not," said Moira. "But I can stop recording if it'll make you more comfortable."

Houseboat only nodded, and Moira paused the recording.

"Thanks," he said. "But no, I don't like Butch. He's hiding something."

"Like what?"

"That's a good question," said Houseboat. "His little island, for one."

"It's not really hidden," said Moira. "I saw it yesterday."

"You saw the outside," said Houseboat. "How many people do you think have been on that island?"

"I don't know," said Moira.

"Butch and his wife," said Houseboat. "If anyone else has, it'd be news to me."

"It is *their* island."

"You spent time with him?"

"I went on a fishing trip with him."

"You're a reporter. You talk to people a lot. What was your read on him?"

"He seemed to be performing," said Moira. "And it was hard to get a read past that."

Houseboat held her gaze for a second and then nodded. "You're smart. That's a good way to describe it. Did he drop it at all?"

"Only when I mentioned Bill Dermott's name."

Houseboat narrowed his eyes. "Hmm. Been gone for almost a week now."

"He dropped it when I mentioned him," said Moira. "But only for a second. Then the facade came back up."

"He's hiding something, Ms. Bell," said Houseboat. "So no, I don't like him. Because I've known him for these past twenty years, and I've never gotten more than a hint of it. Just those little moments, like the one you describe. But never more. He's careful, even if he likes to act a fool. Joan was the one who told you about Bill?"

"Yes," said Moira.

Houseboat sighed. His voice grew quieter, like he was worried about someone listening in. He stared at her.

"What?" asked Moira. "Something wrong?"

"Just thinking," said Houseboat. "Thinking if I can trust you."

"Trust me?" asked Moira. "Trust me with what?"

"I'll tell you, but I've got to do something first," he said. "Can I have your phone?"

Moira eyed him. "You're not going to break it, are you?"

"You'll get it back, I promise," said Houseboat. Moira grabbed it and held it out to him. He took it and walked over to a small cabinet. He opened it, and revealed a safe. HB dialed in the right digits and it opened. He put the phone inside, on top of some other paperwork, and then closed it. Houseboat sat back down, and seemed a little less tense.

"People sometimes just go missing in Blackwell Key," he said, finally.

"What does that mean?"

"I've been here twenty years," said Houseboat. "And a few times a year, a person might disappear. Might not even get reported. *Probably* won't get reported. A husband or wife might take the car or the boat. A kid might wander off. But if you pay attention, you notice it. Over twenty years, dozens and dozens of people. Maybe into triple digits. At least the ones I've noticed, between listening in on the CB, and reading the newspaper, and talking to folks."

"That seems like a crisis."

"It would be," said Houseboat. "But they mostly come back."

Moira raised an eyebrow. "They come back?"

"Yeah," said Houseboat. "After a few days, they come back. Pull back into the driveway, and walk in the front door. Maybe a little confused, but they come back. Ninety-five percent of the time, at least. Sometimes people do stay gone, but most of the time they return."

"And no one talks about it?"

"No," said Houseboat. "No one says a word. Everyone's happy to have their loved one back, usually. Sometimes there's an argument, but mostly it all gets settled down."

"You have proof of this?"

"Cobbled together," said Houseboat. "But some of it is just living here, over the years."

"How many people know about this?" asked Moira.

"Me," said Houseboat. "And you. Over the years, I've tried bringing it up to different people. Subtly, you know. I don't ask right out. But it always gets dismissed out of hand. No questions. No thought."

"Have you taken it to Butch?"

"No," said Houseboat, answering quickly. "Remember what I said about him hiding something?"

"Yeah," said Moira. She studied Houseboat's face. He believed what he said. But she didn't know how much of it she could take on his word alone.

"I'll look into it," she said. "Can I have my phone?"

"Sure," he said, and he grabbed it out of the safe, handing it back to her. It buzzed in her hand, getting reception again outside of the lead safe.

"You're popular," he said.

She looked at her phone. It was a text from Joan.

Bill just walked in the door

Would you come back as soon as you can?

"Jesus," she said.

"What is it?" asked Houseboat.

"Bill Dermott just came back," said Moira.

Houseboat didn't say a word. He just stared at her, zipped up his lips, and threw away the key.

7

Joan sat on her porch again as Moira stepped out of her car. But she wasn't alone. A burly man sat across from her in the other lawn chair, holding a can of Diet Coke, an absentminded smile on his face. Joan's face looked heavy, worse than it had previously, despite her husband's return.

"Joan," said Moira, as she walked up.

"Hi, Ms. Bell," said Joan. "This is my husband, Bill."

Moira extended a hand to Bill, who stared at it for a moment, and then met it, shaking it softly. His skin felt raspy, gritty.

"Nice to meet you," said Moira.

"Nice to meet you, too," said Bill. His voice was low, but soft, each syllable a soft bass.

"I was wondering if you wanted to talk to Bill," said

Joan. "You know, for your story." Moira looked at her, trying to understand her meaning. Joan stared back, fear in her eyes, and Moira thought to Houseboat's words from earlier.

"Oh, sure," said Moira. "Mind if I grab a seat?" Joan gestured to the third patio chair, empty, and Moira grabbed it, positioning it opposite the two of them.

Moira looked to Bill, who took a sip of his soda. His face, in contrast, was light and easy, absent of tension or stress. He looked like he had just gotten a massage.

"How are you, Bill?" asked Moira.

"Oh, I'm alright, I suppose," he said. "I'm glad to be back."

"Where exactly did you go?" asked Moira.

"I don't know," said Bill.

"You don't know?" asked Moira.

"No," said Bill. "Butch found me, out on my boat, drifting."

"What do you remember before that?"

Bill's eyes wandered off into the middle distance, thinking. Moira noticed the smell then, the stink of acrid salt. Her nostrils flared.

"I remember—I remember—I remember having to leave."

"Why did you leave?" asked Moira. "And without telling Joan?"

"I *had* to," said Bill. "It was urgent business, I remember that. I rushed to my boat. It was dark, and the wind was pushing pretty hard, but I needed to go out. I remember that, so distinctly. Fighting the wind. And just this—urgency."

"Why the urgency?" asked Moira.

"I don't know," said Bill. "All I remember is the feeling. I was angry too, but I don't know why. I don't know why I didn't tell Joan. It doesn't make any sense. I would have told her. But I couldn't. So I went out in the dark in my boat."

"And what happened?" asked Moira. Bill's words came out in short sentences, his breath punching them out like bullets.

"Darkness," said Bill, staring off.

"Darkness?" asked Moira. "You were gone for five days, Bill. The sun would have risen."

"I don't remember the sun at all," he said, his voice empty. Moira cast a glance at Joan, and Joan's eyes stared at her husband, and Moira saw the fear in them.

"Do you remember anything else?"

"I remember the water," he said. "I was out on the ocean in the dark, and there was only water. Darkness and water."

"And then Butch found you?" asked Moira.

"Yes," he said, his eyes focusing again. "On our boat. I was behind the wheel, and he hailed me, and I followed him back to land. And then I came back home."

"How do you feel?" asked Moira.

"I feel okay," he said. "Still a little fuzzy around the edges, but generally okay. Glad to be home with Joan." He looked at her and smiled, and it seemed genuine enough to Moira. "Do you have any more questions for me?"

"Not right now," said Moira.

"I think I'm going to work on the boat," said Bill. "Is that okay, sweetheart?"

"Sure," said Joan, mustering a smile. Bill went inside, rustled around for a minute, and then came back out, heading to his truck, and driving away. Joan was silent the entire time, looking down at the ground, a cigarette burning between her fingers. As Bill pulled out, she took a long drag off of it, and let out the smoke in a slow exhale.

"Do you know how Bill and I met?" asked Joan. "I know you don't know. But we met at a bar, down in Key West. Not a lot of places stay open too late on the smaller islands, so I'd go down there. There was a little western bar that had a dance floor, and I'd drink a little and dance. Mostly alone, but sometimes with a guy. But they never liked to dance, they just did it because they wanted to get laid. But then one night, I was nursing a drink and a cigarette, and I see Bill out there on the dance floor, by himself, just scooting and boogying. Dancing by himself."

Another drag on the cigarette. She didn't look at Moira, only down on the ground.

"Now, I thought to myself, that's a handsome man over there, dancing by himself, without a care in the world. And now, I wasn't the only single lady in that bar, so I left my drink and my smoke, and I went and danced with him. And you know that cliché about how time changes when you're with someone special?"

"Yeah."

"Well, it happened with us. We danced, separate at first, but then we touched, and it was like electricity. The music changed, song after song blasting through their stereo, and we kept dancing. Both of us sweated through our shirts, but we didn't care. We just kept going. It felt like we time traveled. An hour later, the music paused, and we both woke up. We got drinks, and we talked. And we had more in common than we knew. Both our daddies had been in the army. Both of us crewed boats. Both of us moved to the Keys for a fresh start. And that vortex extended to us talking, because before we knew it, it was after midnight. And then my ex showed up."

"Bad blood?" asked Moira.

"You could say that," said Joan. "He was a manipulative piece of shit, who always played the victim, no matter how terrible he acted. Kicked him to the curb after one too many fights over something he did he wouldn't apologize for. People make mistakes, mind you, but you have to apologize when you make one. Anyways, he showed up, and he saw us there chatting, and I tried to ignore him, hope he'd go away, and we could vamoose, but he beelined right toward us. Didn't even have a chance to warn Bill about him. Boom, he was right on top of us."

"Did he start a fight?" asked Moira.

"He wanted to," said Joan. "But he didn't want to throw the first punch. He wanted to goad Bill into it. He didn't know Bill and I had just met that night. He thought Bill was my boyfriend. So he just ran up and started calling me every name in the book. Every horrible, awful thing he could think of. Practically frothing at the mouth. And Bill just sat there, eyeing him, and then looking at me. Now I was angry as hell. I had spent the last couple hours with this lovely man, and just as soon as I get something nice, something comes along and ruins it. It's happened my whole life. So I wanted to beat the living hell out of him. They'd be dragging me kicking and screaming away from him. But another part of me didn't want to give him the satisfaction. I just wanted to spend some time with this nice man. Maybe get a kiss and set up another date."

"So what happened?"

"Bill just sat there, and stared at him, as my ex yelled this vile shit. And eventually, my ex ran out of breath, and stopped, put his chin out, waiting for Bill to start something with him. But Bill just sat there and stared at him. Just considered him, no sign of anger or anything on his face, except thought. Finally, he looked over at me."

"He said, 'Well, we found him, Joan. We found the reason.'"

"And now, I was angry, but Bill's response just caught me completely off guard. So I asked him, 'The reason? The reason for what?'"

"And he answered. 'The reason there're more horses' asses in the world than there are horses.' And that caught me off-guard more than before, and I just started laughing, laughing so, so hard. And Bill took a twenty dollar bill, slapped it on the bar, grabbed my hand, and walked me right out of there, right past my ex, who just stood there with his dick in his hand, looking like an idiot. You could have called it then. I never was one for marriage. Always thought I'd be the single spinster aunt. But right then, I knew I'd be marrying this man. And it happened, not even a year later. We were married."

"That's very sweet," said Moira.

"I think about it a lot," said Joan. A single tear had fallen down her cheek, and she wiped it away. "But from that first night, our first date, if you want to call it that, we always had a thing we said to each other whenever someone pissed one of us off. One of us would say they 'found the reason', and the other would ask 'the reason for what?' and then 'the reason there're more horses' asses in the world than there are horses'. You know, like marco polo."

"A call and response," said Moira.

"Yeah, exactly," said Joan. "We've probably done it back and forth ten thousand times. No matter the reason, it was automatic. One of us would start it, and the other would finish. And God, when Bill came back earlier today, you had no idea how pissed I was. When I saw he was okay, I was so angry that he left me without saying a word, and now he comes back, not remembering a single thing. I've been so worried about the past few days, more worried than I'd been about everything. Trying to deal with this goddamn house on my own, and thinking that either he left me for someone else or he just left me because he wanted out, and he didn't even have the goddamn courage to talk to me about it, which isn't like him at all, and a thousand other things running through my head, and I *let him have it.* I know it wasn't the right thing to do, but I couldn't help it. The neighbors probably thought I was going to kill someone. But I had so much pent up emotion, and it all came out, all at once. And Bill, well, he did what Bill usually does when somebody yells at him. He sat there and took it, with a confused look on his face. Bill never expects anyone to yell at him. He thinks it's dumb, you know, to yell. He's never raised his voice to me, not once in almost ten years. Another reason I love him."

"I don't think anyone would blame you," said Moira. "It's a hard thing to go through."

"I know, I know," said Joan. "But nobody is harder on me than me. And as soon as all that came out, I immediately felt guilty. 'Cause I don't think Bill was lying. I truly don't think he remembers any of what happened over these five days, or why he left in the first place. I'd be able to tell if he was lying. Well, normally, I'd be able to tell if he was lying."

"Normally?" asked Moira. "What's different?"

"Well, like I said, I felt guilty about dumping all that on him. So I said it."

"Said what?"

"I said, I think I found the reason," said Joan.

"But this time it was you," said Moira.

"Yeah," said Joan. "This time I was the reason. But Bill didn't answer me. He just stared at me, and didn't say a word."

"Why not?" asked Moira.

"That's a good question," said Joan. "One I've been thinking about. It's why I texted you to come over. You're an outsider, a reporter. You can see things other people can't. And I needed your perspective."

Joan stared at Moira then, her deep eyes lined with worry and anxiety and terror. Another tear rolled down her cheek, but she didn't wipe this one away.

"Because normally, I *could* tell if he was lying. I'd be able to know right off the bat if something was up. That something was wrong with his story—but now, I don't know. I truly don't know."

"Why not?"

"Because—" Joan's voice halted, caught in her throat, and she wiped away the tears and took a long drag on her cigarette, exhaling the smoke slowly. She started again.

"Because I know that man looks just like Bill, and

sounds like him, but it's not him. Whoever that is, it's not my husband. And if it's not my husband, who is it?"

8

"How's Florida?" asked Martin, his voice crackling over the phone for a moment, and then going clear again.

"The Keys aren't really Florida," said Moira. She sat on her balcony, her laptop on the small table in front of her, the ocean crashing just below her.

"You know what I mean," said Martin.

"It's hot," she said.

"Nobody ever accused Florida of being cold," said Martin. He sighed. "Find anything interesting yet?"

"Well, yes," said Moira. "Most of it has very little to do with climate change, though."

"Sometimes that doesn't matter," said Martin. "Sometimes we just need eyeballs, and if we have something juicy, then it doesn't matter if it's not really connected."

"Woman down here name of Joan, who's lost a lot of her house to storm surge from the last hurricane."

"That's related."

"Sure, but the rest isn't," she said. "Her husband left her."

"Husbands do that, occasionally."

"Thanks, smartass," said Moira.

"What would you do without me?"

"I mean, he just left her, like a week ago," said Moira. "Just disappeared, out of the blue. Took their boat and vanished."

"And?"

"And he came back yesterday," said Moira. "Without a single memory of the missing time."

"Amnesia?" asked Martin. "Most of the time that's made up."

"I know," said Moira. "But I believe him. But Joan, she—she told me—no, she *scared* me, talking to me when we were alone."

"Scared you how? You alright?"

"I'm fine," said Moira. "She scared me because she's convinced that whoever came back isn't her husband. It's like a different man altogether."

"I mean, if he had something traumatic happen to him, it could have messed with his memory, and his personality," said Martin. "That's not impossible."

"Something's going on around here, Martin," said Moira. "Something strange. I've got a source that tells me the disappearances are quite common. And that the missing usually come back after a few days. Joan's husband matches it to a tee."

"Are there no police reports about it?"

"No," said Moira. "I looked. Couldn't find anything publicly. But guess who the police chief is?"

"Um, some bozo with a pet alligator," said Martin.

"No," said Moira. "His name is Butch. Butch Blackwell."

"And I'd guess it's not a coincidence that it's Blackwell Key," said Martin.

"No," said Moira. "And he runs the most successful business on the island."

"That's just typical small town corruption, though," said Martin. "Not much different than here, honestly. The mayor here is steeped in it. But that's everywhere."

"Is there a pandemic of people disappearing and then reappearing a week later?"

"Actually," said Martin. "There have been some irregularities I've noticed so far. I dismissed it, honestly. These coastal towns are full of transients and drifters. People come and go all the time."

Martin was in the Chesapeake Bay, where the crab fishing industry had been impacted hard by climate change. They were still reckoning with it.

"These are long-time residents, not random drifters. Something's going on, but I have no idea what. I can't wrap my head around it."

"Well, don't get too involved. That storm looks like it's heading right for you."

"I've been keeping my eye on it," said Moira. "It still could avoid us."

"Last forecast I saw looked like the hurricane had eyeballs, and they were looking at you. It's going to be a big one."

"I'll worry about it when it's closer," said Moira. "I'm close to something here."

"You say that now," said Martin. "But storms down there hit harder. You're surrounded by water. There's no way out once it hits."

"You don't have to remind me," said Moira.

"Sorry," said Martin. "I—I forgot, if you believe that. How are you doing?"

"It's fine," said Moira. "I had a panic attack."

"Jesus, I didn't realize," said Martin.

"I'm okay," said Moira. "I got food poisoning the other night from a casserole at a community potluck."

"Oh god," said Martin. "That sounds terrible."

Visions of inky black hands pulling you under—

"It wasn't great," said Moira. "But otherwise, I've been okay. I knew what I was getting into."

"Unsolved mysteries, apparently," said Martin. "Don't get too deep. We've got a long way to go. I heard from Fran, and she says she can put us in touch with her agent."

"A book deal?" asked Moira.

"Fran says its likely, with our pedigree, and how hot the topic is, right now. No pun intended."

"Well, that's nice. Now we just have to write it," said Moira.

"Well, first we have to get the info. But I've already got some good stuff here. I've gotten in tight with a couple of fishermen."

"Who I assume don't believe in climate change," said Moira.

"You'd assume correctly," said Martin. "But that's part of the intrigue of the story."

"It's—it's just frustrating," said Moira. "They can't see reality when it's happening right in front of their face."

"It's the power of belief," said Martin. "Sometimes seeing something right in front of you isn't enough."

"Fair enough," said Moira. "I'm sure it'll be a theme when we start writing."

"Are you kidding?" asked Martin. "I've already written a thousand words on it."

"You overachiever," said Moira. "You're crazy if you think I've written a single word. Aside from some scribbled notes."

"What's next?" he asked.

"I don't know," said Moira. "I'm going to dig into the missing person issue."

"You think there's something there?" asked Martin. "Seems tangential."

"Everything's connected," said Moira. "This is the thread to pull."

"I trust you," said Martin. "But keep your eyes on that storm, okay? If it comes for you, you have to get out."

"Yes, Dad," said Moira.

"I'm not joking," said Martin.

"I'll be fine," said Moira. "Don't worry about me."

"I'll try my best," said Martin. "I'm going to have some drinks with some crab fishermen."

"Good luck," said Moira. "I'll be in touch." They hung up, leaving Moira alone with the shore.

She had left Joan's the day before unsettled. Joan kept her there, talking, and Moira had quickly realized that Joan didn't want to be alone with Bill after he returned from whatever work he was doing on their boat. She hadn't heard from Joan since, so maybe she had calmed down since her desperate story about Bill's otherness. But Martin was right. If Bill had endured some traumatic experience, he truly could have forgotten all of it, and the same thing could have changed his personality.

Moira thought to the stories she'd read of spouses changing overnight after some happening, of relationships immediately thrown into a wood chipper because of some horrific event.

But was this what that was? What about the scores of other disappearances? Houseboat seemed smart, and he'd definitely been here a long time, long enough to know more than most.

She wiped at her arm, and her fingers came back with a thin layer of salt, one that had been there every time she scratched. No matter how much she showered, the salt was there. She didn't know how the locals could deal with it. It was omnipresent, and no matter how much she tried, the acrid, burning smell of it clung to the inside of her nostrils. Everything tasted like it, no matter how much water she drank. She couldn't escape it.

Moira looked over the water of the late evening. The sun glinted beautifully off of it. She remembered the potluck and the vestiges of the visions she had seen. It hung over her. She had tried to shake it off, to ignore it, but it was still there.

But where did she go from here? Internet research hadn't gotten her very far. There wasn't any news of disappearances on Blackwell Key, at least not the epidemic that Houseboat described. She used Google Earth to get as close to Dagger Key as she could, but even from the sky it was covered. The view only showed a roof of a building, and a large black tarp that covered most of the rest of the ground. Butch was hiding whatever he had there from the eye in the sky. It didn't indict him in anything nefarious, she knew. A lot of people went to extreme lengths to protect their privacy. It didn't make him a monster.

But there was surely something. She didn't need corroboration to believe the fear in Joan's eyes, or in Houseboat's. Or the falseness of Butch's. Something was amiss on Blackwell Key, and she needed to know what it was.

She had to get closer to Butch, but she doubted he'd let her any closer than she'd already gotten. He'd invited her to the potluck, but she didn't think she'd get any closer than that. Deputy Mike, though. That was a thought.

He himself said he had little allegiance to Butch, and he had been willing to give her some information, even with his current job. Maybe she could talk to him. Maybe he could give her another lead.

Her phone buzzed, and she looked to it. An unknown number. She answered it.

"Hello?" she asked.

"Is this Ms. Bell?" asked a male voice.

"Speaking," she said.

"Hi, this is Mike," he said. Speak of the devil.

"Oh, hi," said Moira. "Hey, I was just thinking about you. Sorry for disappearing the other night. My stomach got hit with something real awful. Did anyone else have any stomach trouble that night?"

"No, I don't think so—"

"Because it must have been one of the casseroles. Anyway, I barely made it back to my bed. But I've been meaning to follow up with you. I talked to Houseboat, and you were right, he was a good interview. Gave me some useful information."

"Ms. Bell—"

"And now that Bill has come back, I've only got more questions. I talked to Joan, and she's got me chasing all kinds of threads."

"Ms. Bell—"

"And I know you work for Butch, but I was wondering if you had more time to talk, you know, off-duty?"

"Ms. Bell," he said. "Please, let me get a word in."

"Sorry," said Moira.

"No, it's just—" He paused. She could hear him take a deep breath. "About Joan."

"What about her?" asked Moira.

"Well, we have her down at the station," said Mike. "And I thought you should know, considering how much you've been talking to her."

"At the station?" asked Moira. "Why?"

"Well—" He paused again. "Well, we got a call from her neighbor early, early this morning. Heard some awful screaming coming from their place. So we checked it out."

"And?"

"And—and Bill is dead, Moira. Joan killed him. Chopped him up, into little pieces."

9

Blackwood Key's tiny police station seemed the size of a postage stamp from the outside, tucked away next to the marina.

Wonder if Butch had anything to do with that location.

Mike waited for her inside at the front desk.

"You're here," said Mike, looking visibly shaken. His eyes flitted around, bouncing from her to the floor, to his hands, over and over again. He looked terrible.

"You okay?" asked Moira.

"I'll be alright," said Mike. "Just, never seen anything like that before."

"What happened?"

"Like I said, we rolled in to investigate the screams, and Joan was sitting outside on the front porch, smoking a cigarette, calm as calm could be. She was covered in blood. Looked like she just slaughtered a cow."

"But it wasn't a cow," said Moira.

"No," said Mike. "We tried to ask her what happened, but she hasn't said a single word since we arrested her. Butch tried to talk to her when we got her in, but she refuses to talk."

"And you thought she'd talk to me?"

"Maybe," he said.

"Where's Butch now?"

"He had an emergency. He took the other deputies and flew the coop. Left me to hold down the fort."

"What did she do to Bill?"

"The murder weapon was an axe," said Mike. "And she chopped him up, into just—just meat. Could barely tell it was human."

"Christ," said Moira, wiping her face, a thin dusting of salt coming off in her hand. "Let me talk to her, then."

Mike grabbed a key, and they headed through a door into the back of the station, where their few cells were. Only one was occupied. Joan sat back on the bed, against the concrete wall. A cigarette burned between her fingers. Moira grabbed a folding chair and moved it over to near Joan's cell, just outside the door. Moira nodded at Mike, who went back out to the front area.

Joan took a long drag from her cigarette and blew it out in a plume. She wore the jail house uniform and stared out into the middle distance.

Moira sat there, the room mired in silence.

"It feels like I've been in a nightmare," said Joan, finally. "Ever since Bill went missing. And I keep expecting to wake up. Any moment, I'll jolt back awake in our half a house, and Bill will be there right next to me, sleeping. And I'll hold him, and despite everything, I'll be okay."

She turned to stare at Moira.

"But Bill ain't coming back," said Joan. "And there ain't no waking up from this."

"What happened, Joan?" asked Moira. "Why did you do it?"

She stared at Moira. "That wasn't Bill," said Joan. "I told you—"

"Sometimes, people go through traumatic events, and it can alter their memory, alter their personality. You don't know what happened—"

"That wasn't Bill," said Joan, her voice cold and dry. "You didn't see what I saw."

"What did you see?" asked Moira.

"After you left the other day, he came back," said Joan. "And—" she paused, and she took a deep breath. "—and I could almost pretend life was back to normal again. Bill was there, doing his normal routines. Sure, sometimes he seemed out of it. He wasn't responding to everything normally. But like you said, maybe something bad happened to him out there, and he was having trouble. I tried to compartmentalize it, I tried, Moira, I tried so hard—"

Joan's voice hitched in her throat, and she paused, taking a long breath, and then a long drag on the cigarette. Then she was calm again.

"But last night—last night I woke up, and I was alone again. Bill wasn't in bed, and he wasn't in the bathroom, and it didn't matter how he acted or what he did. All I knew in that moment was that he had vanished again. He had left, for whatever reason, and it felt like a nightmare. You ever have a nightmare that just keeps looping? Like Groundhog Day?"

"Recursive, you mean?" asked Moira.

"I guess so," said Joan. "It felt like that. Like the past week had just been a nightmare, and now I was going to live through it again, and again, and again. And my heart was racing, immediately into fight-or-flight mode. I needed to know what happened to Bill. I looked out front, to the driveway, and Bill's truck was still there, and so was my car, and that calmed me down a little. If he went anywhere, it was on foot."

"Why would he go anywhere at all?" asked Moira.

"I wasn't thinking straight," said Joan. "But whatever. I just stopped for a second, and I listened. Because of the state of the house, I just got kind of used to a certain amount of outside noise. Road sounds, birds, bugs, what have you. And that was there, but there was something else. Another noise, coming from behind the house. And I didn't know what it was. It sounded like—like a low glugging noise. It didn't make any sense. So I went to check on it. I thought I'd find Bill."

"What did you find?" asked Moira.

"I found—I found—" Joan stopped again.

"Joan?"

"Remember how I told you that whoever had come back wasn't my husband?"

"Yes," said Moira.

"I didn't find Bill," said Joan. "Because Bill is dead, and probably has been for a week now. What I found in the backyard was what replaced him. And it wasn't human."

"Wasn't human? What are you talking about?" asked Moira.

"I crept to the back of the house, and looked outside, and I saw the thing that was using Bill as a mask."

"I don't—"

"It wasn't Bill anymore, not completely. It transformed back, closer to its true form, or what I'd guess is its true form. What it really looks like, when it's not wearing someone else's skin. I could still see Bill in there, somewhere, around the edges. His features were still present, somewhat. It was naked. It made sense."

"What did it look like?" asked Moira.

"Grayish silver, and soft, and wet. Like a fish, or a sea slug. It was halfway to human, but that made it worse. I remember its feet. It didn't have toes, just fins, and its skin, its skin was drooping, melting almost—I couldn't breathe."

"You had heard a noise," said Moira.

"It was drinking," said Joan. "Or maybe breathing. It was hard to tell. Its mouth was different, big, wider, the jaw expanding like a snake, or a whale, gulping in sea water."

"What was it drinking?" asked Moira.

"I—I don't know," said Joan. "It was in a bucket, one of the buckets from the boat. I assumed that's what he'd gotten when he'd gone back to the boat. But I don't know how. It was—it was black. And thick, and it stank. Stank like rotted seawater, like a long dead fish corpse, split open on the beach. It looked like tar, like the darkest ocean water, but it wasn't either, and the thing was dumping it down its gullet, gulping it down—"

Joan stopped then, and she wiped the tears away from

her face.

"And it was obvious, right away, but this thing killed my husband and took his place. And I was so scared, by whatever this horror was, just terrified, but then all of it went away, replaced by this sudden rage. It stood there, swallowing gallons of that dark sludge, pretending to be my husband, and everything turned red. There was an axe outside, and I pushed the door open and grabbed it, and the thing started screaming, wailing, this horrible, inhuman noise, and I started swinging as hard as I could. It didn't stop screaming, even as I cut into it. I—"

"It's okay," said Moira.

"No," said Joan. "I started screaming too, as I hit it, over and over again, and soon it stopped. Its blood went everywhere, and I'm sure some went into my eyes, but I didn't stop. I swung and swung and swung, until my shoulders and hands and forearms ached, up and over and over. Until I couldn't anymore. I couldn't breathe, and I couldn't see, and then I stopped, and reality came back, and the creature was gone."

"You killed it," said Joan.

"But now it was Bill again," said Joan. "The thing, the thing I killed, it had transformed back. And it looked like Bill, and I dropped the axe, and I went and smoked a cigarette. The cops showed up."

"Are you sure you saw what you saw?" asked Moira.

"I know it sounds crazy," said Joan. "I know it does. But I know Bill. Knew him." She paused. "That wasn't him. And I didn't need to see that thing in my yard to know it. But I couldn't stand by and let it keep pretending it was him. I'd rather rot in hell." Joan stared at Moira, and Moira read her, and saw that Joan believed everything she said. There was not an ounce of deceit in her eyes. And Moira remembered what Houseboat had told her.

"Joan," said Moira. "Have you noticed a disproportionate amount of people going missing on Blackwell Key?"

Joan looked down at the concrete floor. "No one talks about it," she said, after a beat.

"Houseboat told me," said Moira.

"He would," said Joan, cracking a smirk for the first time since Moira had stepped into the room. "If you mention it to most people, they just call you crazy, or ignore you, or change the subject. But it's impossible not to notice. At least once a month."

"But you stayed," said Moira.

"We had nowhere to go," said Joan. "And eventually, when everyone tells you something is normal, you stop questioning it. The house is on fire, and everyone's still slow dancing."

Moira's mind whirled. She still had so many questions.

"You're thinking it too, aren't you?" asked Joan.

"Thinking what?" asked Moira.

Joan laughed, a dark, joyless laugh. She leaned back against the cold concrete and stared at Moira. "About all those missing people. About all those people who came back. They disappear for a day or two or five, and then, boom, they're back, and everything's back to normal. Like Bill. Bill came back five days later, and everything was supposed to be hunky dory, except me and my axe decided I wasn't going to keep dancing."

She laughed again, and then cut it off, a terrible look in her eye. "I know it's a hard thought. Because there's a part of me that wants to deny it. It wants me to think that I just went crazy, and killed my poor husband, chopped him up in the backyard. Because that's simpler. That's just me and him. But I know it ain't true. I know Bill went missing, and five days later, that thing came crawling back. And it isn't the first time it's happened. Because I think that's what's happened every time. All those missing people, they all got replaced. And those shape-shifting bastards are everywhere, all among us. Hiding in plain sight."

"I—I can't believe that," said Moira. The thought was crazy.

"You're a good reporter," said Joan. "And you want proof. Well, I know where you'll find it."

"Where?"

"Butch kept asking me to talk," said Joan. "And I didn't say a word. Not a peep. But I watched him, and I listened to the questions he asked. And he knows, Moira. He knew it wasn't Bill."

"I—what makes you think that?"

"It was one question he asked," said Joan. "After I hadn't answered any for a while, and kept peppering me with them. He asked 'why did you kill them?' And let me tell you something, Moira, it won't come as much of a shock to you, but Butch Blackwell ain't much for gender neutral pronouns. Why would he ask me that? Unless he knew what it was. That it had no gender, 'cause it wasn't one of us." She stared right into Moira, her eyes boring a hole in her. "They are all around us, Moira. Most of the island, at this point. And Butch is doing all he can to hide it."

"But why?" asked Moira.

"I don't know," said Joan. "But I know that if you want

evidence, it's on Dagger Key. Visit the island. Butch did something to Bill. I know it."

10

Butch met her as she left the police station, with his two other deputies in tow.

"Well, Ms. Bell," said Butch, that same implacable smile on his face, looming over her. "Didn't expect to see you here."

"I invited her, Butch," said Mike. "I thought Joan may talk if it was with Ms. Bell, instead of one of us."

Butch glanced at him, and raised his eyebrows, and then back to Moira. "Well, did it? Get anything out of her, Ms. Bell?" He eyed her, blocking her only exit to the police station. Moira looked to him, and the other two deputies, who also looked at her.

"No," she said, finally. "No, she wouldn't talk to me. I tried my best."

Butch eyed her, his eyes narrowing, even as the wide smile remained. "You wouldn't happen to know anything else that would help the investigation, would you? I know you'd been spending a lot of time over at the Dermott house."

"I don't think so, Butch," said Moira. "I'll be sure to help you if anything relevant comes up." Silence hung in the air around them.

"I appreciate that, Ms. Bell," said Butch. "Be seeing you." And he tipped his hat, and they walked past her, and the acrid smell of salt surrounded her, and the deputies' faces blurred in her peripheral vision, and she looked to them, but their faces were normal again.

She glanced once to Mike, softly nodded, and left.

*

"Houseboat, you home?" she asked, walking up the empty dock toward his floating house.

"Yeah, I'm here," he said, popping out from inside. He wore ratty jeans and a denim vest over a bare chest. His long hair was tied into a bun on top of his head. "I heard what happened to Joan over the police band."

"I just came from the police station."

"You can come aboard," said Houseboat. "Let's go inside, away from prying eyes."

She stepped over, eyeing the thin gap of water between the dock and the deck. Houseboat went inside and she followed him in. The ship in a bottle still lay in pieces at his workstation.

"I haven't made a lot of progress on it," he said. "Haven't been able to focus lately." The radio played weather updates.

"How's the storm looking?" asked Moira.

"Worse and worse," said Houseboat. "Fewer and fewer potentialities that don't end in apocalypse. It's heading right for us."

"Scary fucking storm," said a voice from a corner of the room, and Moira jumped.

"Fucking hell," she said, reflexively. She looked to the voice and recognized the source. It was the same ratty dude she'd seen walking past the first time she'd visited.

"Sorry," said the man. "Didn't mean to scare you."

"This is my friend, Zeb," said Houseboat. "Zeb, this is Moira. Zeb was just leaving."

"What? Come on—"

"We have private business to discuss," said Houseboat.

"She's the reporter, right? What's going on?" asked Zeb, looking at Houseboat. He glanced at her. "Why did Joan do it?"

"Zeb, please," said Houseboat.

"I can help," said Zeb, looking at Moira. "I know everybody, everybody on the island. I've got contacts, I've got some good dirt—"

"Zeb," said Houseboat, his voice as stern as Moira had heard it. "If we need your help, we'll contact you." Zeb looked to Houseboat one more time with pleading eyes, met only resistance, and then walked out past Moira, winking at her as he passed. Houseboat waited as Zeb's footsteps faded as he walked down the dock.

"Your friend?" asked Moira.

"Well, acquaintance," said Houseboat.

"Does he really know things?" asked Moira. "Another source for what's going on around here—"

"It's best not to involve Zeb unless we absolutely have to," said HB. "Things tend to get messy around him."

He sat down, and Moira sat down in the same seat as before. She reached into her purse and handed him her phone, as a matter of course. He winked at her and locked it up.

"You talk to Joan?"

"Yes," said Moira.

"Butch let you?"

"Butch didn't know about it," said Moira. "Mike let me in while Butch was away on an emergency. Don't know what the hell kind of emergency would take him away from a murder suspect who butchered her husband, but whatever. Gave me some time."

"That Mike fella isn't half bad," he said.

"He's not in Butch's pocket," said Moira. "At least he doesn't seem to be. But Joan hadn't said a word to them."

"I don't blame her," said Houseboat. "Did she do it?"

"Yes."

"Jesus," said Houseboat, rubbing his face.

"Chopped him up with an axe," said Moira. "But—but her story, I can't—"

"What is it?" asked Houseboat. "Tell me."

Moira told him Joan's story, down to the letter. Houseboat sat and listened without interruption.

"Do you believe her?" asked Houseboat.

"I don't know," said Moira. "*She* believed it, though. She wasn't lying, or embellishing."

"Who on Earth would invent a story like that?" asked

Houseboat. "At this point—" He stopped, cutting himself off.

"What?"

"At this point, most of the population of this island would be one of those missing folk," he finished. "Most of the people here aren't people at all. They're those creatures. Voidborn."

"What'd you say? What'd you call them?"

"Voidborn," said Houseboat. "The way you described it. Or Joan did. It felt like an old story I read in a pulp magazine. These creatures came out of the darkness and ate it to survive."

"It wasn't darkness it was eating," said Moira. "It was some kind of briny tar substance."

"Close enough for me," said Houseboat. "But I don't know—"

"Something strange is going on," said Moira. "But believing the whole island is taken over by those things is a stretch."

"I'll give any ole' idea the time of day," said Houseboat. "And if I can't find any evidence, I'll discard it. And I don't have any problem with Joan. Or Bill, for that matter."

"But this is too crazy?" asked Moira.

Houseboat looked at her. "Weren't you here about climate change?"

"You pull on threads and see what unravels."

"Or you toss in a line and see what bites?"

"I guess," said Moira. "But you yourself said something is up with Butch's island. You were suspicious about the missing people. Ever since I've been here—"

She stopped herself this time.

"What is it?" asked Houseboat.

"Ever since I've gotten here, I've been seeing things. Feeling things. Things at the edge of my vision. People's faces, they blur and change. I got sick at the potluck, and felt awful, and remembered going into the water. Getting pulled down. It reminded me of when I was a kid. When—"

Houseboat stared at her. "When what?"

"When I drowned," she said. "Got pulled out by a riptide up near Vero Beach on vacation and—and I drowned. I was dead for ten minutes. A lifeguard revived me."

"Part of the club," said Houseboat. "I was nineteen. Hit my head on the side of the boat, and got knocked unconscious in the water. They pulled me out a minute later. Had about a gallon of water in my lungs. But they brought me back."

"And you live on the water?" asked Moira. "Don't think I could do that."

"I never go in it," he said with a sad smile.

"But it brought up those memories. It felt so real."

"You said it felt like you were being pulled down?"

"Yeah," she said, thinking. "By inky blackness. Something in the water. And I couldn't resist it. A part of me *wanted* to get pulled down."

"A siren's song," he said. "The call of the abyss." Houseboat looked out over the water. "I hear it sometimes."

"How?"

"It's in my memories," he said. "I'm down there in the water, but I'm not alone. There's something down there with me. Something—" He took a deep breath. "Something I don't have the words for. But it's there, and it wants to embrace me. It wants to keep me there. And I know, I know I got out of the water. I got pulled out and brought back. But in my memories, I don't want to be taken out. I want to stay down there, forever." He shivered. "It terrifies me."

"Have you seen anything else?"

"No," said Houseboat. "Nothing outside of healthy skepticism."

"I need to go to Dagger Key," said Moira. "I want to see what Butch is hiding. I don't know if Joan saw what she saw, but she's right. If there's evidence, that's where it's hiding."

"How good of a swimmer are you?" asked Houseboat.

"I'm a fantastic swimmer," said Moira. "I'm just terrified of the water."

"Well, I can get you close," said Houseboat. "Sounds travels on the water, so he'll hear the engine if we try and dock near the shore. Maybe if we get close and paddle in. Either way, you'll have to finish the trip swimming."

"So you're in?"

"Of course," said Houseboat. "Been wanting to get to the bottom of it for years now. Finally got some help. Can you handle the water?"

"I'll have to, if that's what it takes," said Moira. The thought made her heart race. She took a deep breath.

"You sure?"

"I need proof of something," said Moira. "You pull a thread, and see what unravels."

"You say that now," said Houseboat. "That's before we're out there. And before you're down in the water, down with the sirens. And that's not counting if we get caught trespassing on Butch's island."

"I've been arrested before."

"Ha," said Houseboat. "I have, too. But I have a feeling that we aren't going to jail if Butch catches us. I suspect we'll be two more people who just disappear for a week or so and then come back, without a question or a thought."

"I have people who will check up on me," said Moira. "And will investigate if I go missing."

"It's probably why Butch keeps an eye on you," said Houseboat. "He can't control you, not like most other people here."

"Anything I need?"

"I'd get yourself a wetsuit," said Houseboat. "And a waterproof bag to take anything with you. I've got a waterproof camera you can use."

"I can do that," she said. "You think Joan is safe in jail?"

"No, probably not," said Houseboat. "If even a little bit of what she said is true, she's a huge liability to whatever he's planning."

"What *is* he planning?" asked Moira. "He already has control over the entire island."

Houseboat exhaled through his nose and looked at his hands. "How much philosophy do you read?"

"Not very much," said Moira. "Only enough to be dangerous."

Houseboat chuckled. "Okay. How much about alien life, or about possible alien contact?"

"I read Sphere once," said Moira. "Most of my non-fiction reading is about climate change."

"I read a lot about aliens, and possible contact," said Houseboat. "I know, I know, you're shocked. But a thing every thinker and writer brings up is about our preconceptions about thought, and about ways of thinking. Most humans just want to live a happy life. What that means might change, but it's a safe assumption for most."

"But creatures that arose on a different planet, or ecosystem, or culture might be so fundamentally different that we can't understand them," said Moira.

"Right," said Houseboat. "Not that complicated. At least in theory. But these things, if Joan is right, and they're throughout the island—what Butch is planning, or what they are planning, might not be the right questions. Any question at all might not be adequate. We might not be able to grasp how or why they do *anything*. These creatures, whatever they are, or wherever they come from, might be out of our grasp."

"Butch seems human to me," said Moira. "I've met plenty of men like him."

"We'll know when we get you on that island."

"When do we go?"

"Well, pitch dark's about midnight, and so we've got seven hours," said Houseboat. "Enough time to eat dinner and get you a wetsuit."

"Tonight?"

"No time like the present."

11

They paddled in the dark.

Houseboat had steered them as close as he dared, but Dagger Key was still small in the distance, almost invisible under the partial moon. She could see the swaying cypress trees, barely visible. He grabbed an oar for each of them, and they began paddling. The boat was large, but they still made progress, the wind blowing with them.

"I feel exposed out here," said Moira.

"Not many people out at night," said Houseboat. "And if someone saw us, they'd probably leave us alone."

"Unless it was Butch," said Moira. "Doubt he'd leave us alone, paddling in the dark toward his island."

Moira focused on the movement of her oar, doing her best to not let the ocean surrounding them overwhelm her. She'd have to get into it soon, and the anxiety was already building inside her. She pushed it away, pulling on the water with every stroke, the dark cypress trees slowly getting bigger and bigger.

They had waited until after midnight, until true dark, as Houseboat had called it. Moira had tried to nap after dinner, so that'd she'd be fresh for her swim, but she couldn't sleep, the anxiety snapping her awake whenever she drifted off. Houseboat had cooked her dinner, some chicken and yellow rice.

"You ever done anything like this before?" asked Moira.

"No, not really," said Houseboat. "I try not and start fights. For a long time, I thought that was the best way. Live and let live, you know. But lately, I've been thinking that maybe I should have started some ruckuses when it bared doing."

"Some things are worth fighting over," said Moira.

"You're right," said Houseboat. "I kind of abandoned that with my old life, to be truthful."

"Do you ever miss it?"

"Oh, not really," said Houseboat. "I had a lot of money and power, but it was killing me. I miss some of the people, once in a while. But I did have drive, you know? I had ambition. I—I cared about things."

"It's easy to get comfortable," said Moira.

"You're not wrong," said Houseboat. "This sure as hell isn't comfortable. Butch is going to take our heads if he sees us."

Moira wasn't worried about her head with Butch. Everything about him was obscured, in the dark, and Moira knew that if they got caught, physical harm was low on the list of her worries. She'd find the answer on Dagger Key. A part of her already pulled away from whatever that answer was.

Maybe it's nothing but a fire pit and some lawn chairs, a place for him to drink beer away from everyone else.

But she didn't believe that. Not after what Joan saw. And after years of investigating, and dozens of stories, Moira knew you always trace the trouble in a place to the top. It always came back around.

"I think this is about as close as we should get," said Houseboat.

"You sure?" asked Moira. She looked out over the dark water, gently lapping against the side of the boat. They had drawn much closer, but the distance between them and the island still seemed near infinite.

"Might hear us if we get any closer," said Houseboat. "Sound travels easy on the water. Even the oars. And if we want to get away without being seen or heard—"

"Okay," said Moira, taking a deep breath. "I'm going to change." She ducked inside into the bathroom and changed into the wetsuit.

"You ready?" asked Houseboat as she emerged. He held out goggles, and she grabbed them, sliding them onto her head.

"No," she said. "But I'm doing it, anyway."

"If something goes wrong, scream like you're on fire," said Houseboat. "I'll come as fast as I can."

Moira nodded, but didn't think her screaming would do any good. She wanted to scream right now at the thought of jumping into the water. It waited for her, dark in the night, grasping at her, pulling at her.

Houseboat opened a small gate, giving her access to the side of the boat. She sat down and dangled her feet in the water. Moira took deep breaths, closing her eyes, focusing only on her air. She pushed the goggles over her eyes and slid into the cool night water.

Her heart rate escalated, thumping in her chest and in her ears, and bobbed, breathing deeply until it slowed again. She could handle this. She *would* handle this.

"I'll be right here when you come back," said Houseboat. "Be careful."

Moira nodded, took one final deep breath, and dove under the water, swimming a foot down and away from the boat, heading toward Dagger Key.

The water wasn't deep here, only twenty feet at deepest, but the slim light of the moon didn't penetrate more than a foot, and only darkness lay beneath her. Her heart beat hard in her chest, but no hands reached up to grab her, and no riptides pulled at her. The water slid easily underneath her hands and feet. Moira swam soundlessly just below the surface, doing her best to stay silent.

She focused only on her breathing, meditating as she swam. As thoughts intruded, she acknowledged them and pushed them away, returning to her breathing, and the movement of her body as she moved through the water. She hadn't lied to Houseboat; she *was* a good swimmer. Moira had avoided the water for a long time after her accident, but had overcompensated in her early twenties, taking long lessons at the local Y, swimming lap after lap, thinking it would help her overcome her fear. She had done everything to show how powerful she was. There were self-defense classes, MMA and jiu-jitsu. There was the pistol she bought and learned how to shoot, that she'd told no one about. It still sat in the drawer next to her bed in her apartment in the Bronx. Anything to drive away the fear.

Moira didn't fear swimming in a lap pool anymore, but the water itself was never the problem. It was the sea, the deep, the endless expanse of water, and what it represented. An infinite well of chaos and unpredictability. But she let none of those thoughts enter her head as she pushed the water away and drew closer to Dagger Key.

Suddenly her feet hit something, and she gasped, and then she realized it was the sea floor, the water now shallow enough for her to walk, chest deep. She was close now, close enough to hear the wind rustle through the cypress trees. Moira stood, and pulled the goggles down, hanging around her neck as she walked toward the island.

A slim stretch of sand separated the wall of cypress trees from the water, some encroaching past it, and Moira stepped out of the water, happy to leave it behind her. She stopped, kneeling, listening to the sounds of the island, and the water. She didn't see anything but the water and the trees. Her eyes had adjusted over the past hour, and she could see better, but darkness lay beyond the cypress trees, the thick canopy blocking out the small amount of light from the moon and stars.

But she heard something, a small sound, rhythmic and strange. Something she couldn't recognize, and it came from deeper in the island, past the trees.

She hadn't come here to just stand on the shore, and she stepped past the fibrous roots, pushing through the dense cover they provided. It was dark as midnight again, but she could still hear the noise, the weird sound, unearthly and alien, and she walked toward it, each foot stepping out with caution, feeling for purchase. The sound got louder and louder, and she realized it was voices. But they spoke a language she had never heard before, a deep guttural noise, with snarls and clicks, the sound of choking. The sound of a windpipe closing.

Fear grew inside her, but she focused her breath again, easy and free, her heart beating harder, and not only with fear, but also with excitement. There was something here, something strange, and she would find out what it was and break the story. The thrill of the hunt was there right alongside that fear, and Moira reached inside and grabbed it, relished in it. She pushed through the thick brush.

The sounds grew louder, and then Moira saw a glimpse of light through the brush, and she went toward it. The light flickered through the leaves, but she chased it, trying to stay as silent as possible as the rhythmic sounds of choking, of gurgles, of unearthly noise got louder and louder.

Moira slowed as she pushed through the thin trees and brush, the light becoming brighter and brighter. The orange light grew and shrank, and Moira now saw that it came from torches. The fires burned bright, casting light over the whole area. She ducked down into the brush, staying as still as possible. She saw it all.

The area was open, the dark tarp that covered the interior of the island gone now, pulled back to one side. The sky sat above them, a mirror of the sea below. Butch was there, as well as the two deputies that weren't Mike. She didn't know their names. They stood within a circle, surrounded by the torches, wearing black robes. The circle was comprised of plain white stone, limestone, common in the Keys, Moira thought at first. But then she looked closer and realized they stood on salt. Mostly ground fine, but with larger chunks as well, scattered about. But her eyes only glimpsed it, because they were drawn to the center of the circle, where Butch and his two men stood in a triangle around it.

It was an obelisk, black, standing ten feet tall, jutting out of the ground. Its darkness contrasted against the white salt at their feet. A dark basin lay on the ground at its base, a dark concave circle, standing to separate the white and the black. She'd never seen anything like it, the standing stone, if it was stone at all. It sparkled in the flickering light of the orange torches, tapering into a fine point above the heads of the three men.

The sounds came from them, erupting from their throats and mouths, the dark noise filling the area, echoing. As the sound washed over her, she felt her stomach turn, and Moira swallowed down bile that leapt into her throat. Snarls, whips, gurgles, growls, tumbled out of them, forming into words for the damned. It was hellish, and she dug her fingernails into her palms, trying to avoid listening to it. They entered her ears and ate her from the inside.

What was this? Some sort of ritual?

She'd never seen an obelisk like this. Butch and the deputies wore black robes, their hoods pulled back, their arms outstretched toward the stone. The sounds coming from them got louder and louder. Moira couldn't ignore it, couldn't push the sounds away. The men were speakers, dictating in alien violence, and she was going to scream, she couldn't help it, and it got louder, and then they stopped.

Moira opened her eyes, realizing that she had closed them in the first place, and Butch approached the monstrous tower, the black creation, and stood just outside the basin. And then Moira saw the pool was not empty, but was filled with liquid. Butch pulled a slim dagger from a pocket or a belt somewhere and held it for a moment before sliding it across each forearm, blood instantly running in rivulets, dropping into the salt.

What the fuck? He would bleed to death.

Then the two deputies were at his side, and they had handfuls of the white salt, and they rubbed it into his wounds, and Butch spoke again, the dark exhalations of violent sound coming louder now, louder than possible, a human voice couldn't create such sound, but still it came, and the blood poured out, mixing with the salt, and Butch dropped to his knees in front of the basin, and sunk his arms into the black liquid, all the while singing the alien song.

And then he stopped, but only to scream. The dark liquid bubbled and he shook, and then finally pulled his arms out. But they were clean, unmarked, the wounds created by the blade gone.

He rose to his feet and stood back, all three of them watching as the liquid bubbled and gurgled.

And Moira saw then, saw that the basin was not shallow, but was infinite. That it touched the ocean's depths, somehow, some way, it contained the water from a thousand seas, deeper than deep. And Butch had plunged his bloody, salted wounds into it, into the deepest part of the water, and brought it to the surface.

And then it rose before them, and Moira saw what Joan had seen.

A dark creature, soft from living in the deep, dark sea, under thousands of pounds of pressure. Its skin was viscous and sallow, gleaming under the light of the torches. It pulled itself out from the basin and stood on two unsteady legs, standing on dry land for the first time. Its eyes were massive, dominating its face, its mouth slim and lipless, gasping for breath, its skin drying as she watched.

Dark toxic sludge dripped from its fingers, and the white salt below it absorbed it all.

Moira felt the bile rise again in her throat, felt the tension and fear in her stomach build. This thing didn't belong here, called from a place unreachable by man. And yet it stood there. Butch had summoned it.

But why?

And then she saw. It changed, transformed, its sallow, oily skin changing, shifting. Its strange, malformed, fish-like body changed into something more familiar, a shape that Moira recognized.

One of a man.

Within a minute, the awful thing had transformed completely, now looking like an average-looking man of both height and build.

It stared at Butch for a moment and took its first breath.

12

The man—

Not a man, something else, something deep

The man walked away with Butch and the deputies, the ceremony over and already forgotten, all of them walking like they were going to drink a beer and watch some football, but they had instead *pulled* that thing from somewhere deep and misbegotten and unreachable, but Butch had found a way, with the dark monolith of salt and blood and touched the thing below.

Moira finally stopped holding it and vomited in the brush, throwing up what was left of Houseboat's cooking onto the ground. She wiped her face as best she could and hurried to the shore. She had to get back, she had to tell Houseboat.

Moira pushed through the brush, heading to the sound of the water, away from that thing, away from that dark ritual. The cypress trees were dark, but they weren't as dark as the water in the basin, the basin that reached to the bottom of a well so deep and dark that no man had touched it

Aside from Butch.

Moira pushed, moving by feel alone, the night dark still filling the space beneath the leaves of the cypress trees. Her nostrils burned from the bile and acid she had thrown up, but there was something else burning inside her, the knowledge of that thing, the impossible thing.

But you know it's not alone. Bill was one of those things, and there's more of them. Houseboat said there had been hundreds.

Moira pushed the thought away for now. She still had to swim back, still had to face the water again. She reached the slim stretch of sand on the edge of Dagger Key, and if she squinted, she saw the silhouette of the boat far away. It didn't seem that far while she was swimming.

Moira stared at the water. She could do this. She had swam out here, she could swim back.

Breathe deep, Moira. Breathe deep.

She took a deep breath, and pushed it out, and with it, forced out all the thoughts, trying to think of nothing but her breath. Let the thoughts of everything be gone, be gone until she could spend the time to think about them. They wouldn't serve her here. She breathed until she was empty of everything but breath, and then stepped into the water, pulling the goggles over her eyes.

She waded out, the water slowly growing deeper, and

Moira continued to breathe as she walked out into the dark, dark water. The thought of that thing that emerged from the blood and salt kept popping into her mind, and its transformation into a man, hiding in plain sight. The thought kept returning, no matter how much breath she breathed, felt it pull into her body and back out, but the thought wouldn't leave, wouldn't leave. She swam, not caring if she was splashing, if the noise was too much. Moira swam hard for Houseboat. She needed out of the water, she needed to get back.

The boat was getting closer, she could see it, but the water felt heavy, and no matter how much she breathed, no matter how much she focused on her air, the thoughts kept intruding, the thoughts of that thing underneath the water, reaching for her, pulling at her, its not quite hands stretching up to grab her ankles and pull her below the waves where she would never be alone again.

Moira swam hard, imagining herself in that lap pool, pushing, pushing, her legs and shoulders kicking and pulling as hard as she could, but she slowed. The water was heavy.

More than heavy. It was the thing below. Filled and nourished by blood and salt and toxic death, black sludge pouring from somewhere else, death made form, other made form. Something unrecognizable, and it was with her.

I'm going to drown again. I'm going to die here.

A hand grabbed her, and she was a child again.

"Don't go out too deep," said her mom, but she didn't listen, and *no, please no, I don't want to be trapped in this.*

But she knew better, she was a child, and she knew how

to swim, and the water felt great, cool underneath the hot Florida sun. They were vacationing, and Moira had never swam in the ocean before, but she took right to it, it was so much better than the pool. The pool was fine, but it wasn't real, it wasn't alive. Stepping out into the waves felt like exploring. It felt dangerous. Tiny little Moira stepped out, her slight frame being bombarded with waves, but she laughed with each one, even as it would knock her over, and she would climb up, out of the surf, and get hit again. Her parents watched her, worried at first, but then realizing she was fine, she was small, but strong. She was a good swimmer.

Then they stopped watching, turning to their books, and little Moira went deeper, in search of her limit, testing herself. She always did as a child, and then into adulthood, pushing herself to the limit, and sometimes past. It explains the stitches, the broken bones, the scars from rock climbing, from parasailing, from her boxing and jiu-jitsu lessons. It started with her as a child, and so she went out deeper.

First to her waist and then to her chest, and then most children would turn back, afraid of the power of the ocean, but her parents hadn't warned her about riptide, simply didn't know about it, and so she thought she could always swim back whenever it got too deep, got too scary.

And then it was to her neck, and Moira looked back and saw her parents were still on the shore, and it seemed a million miles away. She waved, but they didn't wave back, they were reading, enjoying some quiet time on the beach. And she turned back, and the wave went over her head, and up her nose, and the salt burned at her sinuses.

Fear popped into her heart then, as she reached for the bottom and she couldn't find it with her toes, and another wave washed over her head, and she went under, and took a moment to get back to the surface.

But she did, and took a quick breath, and started swimming back to the shore, as hard as her little feet would kick, as her small shoulders could paddle. But the riptide sapped at her, fighting her with every stroke. No matter how hard she swam, she made little progress. It felt like a nightmare. It felt impossible. She knew she was capable, but it didn't matter, the ocean erased her progress, too big, too strong, impossible to fight, no matter how much energy she had, no matter how much determination and struggle, no matter how much spirit, the ocean would always win, indefatigable, invincible.

Moira swam hard, and the tide fought against her, and it pushed her back, and she looked toward the ocean, and saw something as the water receded, something hiding underneath the surface. Something viscous, with sallow skin, massive dead eyes and a slim, lipless mouth. More than one. Two, three, and she knew there were more there, dozens of them, waiting for her, with loose skinned arms, coated in salt and blood and unearthly darkness, sludge that would burn at the touch.

This is impossible, they weren't there—

But they were there, they are always there, always lurking beneath the water, waiting in the deep. They are old, older than time, older than the Earth, and they have waited, waited so, so long to come back. They were banished once, sleeping, waiting for welcoming arms to call for them again, to sound the trumpets that would herald their arrival, so of course they were there, and they reached out for little Moira as she kicked, and they grabbed her ankles. Their sickly, soft skin touched, seized her, their scales rubbing against the flesh.

She kicked, hard, trying to escape, but their flesh stuck to her, the toxic sludge melding them, keeping her there, and as she fought they dragged her under the water, she was so tiny; she didn't have a chance, and she sputtered, sputtered.

They aren't here, this is mine, not theirs, they—

But the intrusion of logic and thought couldn't survive, not with them. Their presence occluded any of that, and they infiltrated it all, throughout time and space and memory. It was too late.

They pulled on her ankle, dragging her underwater, and she tried to hold her breath, but her lungs couldn't hold, and she breathed, breathed in salt water.

And that was the worst, because it was a new pain. It always ended here, with darkness and a presence.

But not now.

Now she saw them, and they carried her, a boon and bounty underneath the water. Except she was not a slave, not a captive. She went willingly with them, as they all would. They would welcome them with open arms, bleeding fresh with salted wounds. The creatures would walk arm in arm with her, down below, her life as a child far behind her, and they would greet the creatures' lord and master together.

And Moira walked with them on the bottom of the sea, the dark sand between her toes, and she breathed nothing but salt water.

A hand grabbed her, and she sputtered.

"Moira, Moira!" yelled Houseboat, with as loud a voice as he could warrant, in troubled waters.

She opened her eyes to find herself on the deck of Houseboat's vessel.

"You're safe," he said, and she coughed, coughed, and threw up salt water, her eyes and nose burning, her goggles were gone, lost somewhere in the water. "You're on my boat."

"I—I saw—"

"What did you see?" asked Houseboat.

"I saw them," said Moira. "I saw them. Both here, and there."

"Slow down, Moira," he said. "Take a second. What did you see?"

"I saw what Joan described," said Moira. "She was telling the truth. I saw the Voidborn."

13

"—Tropical Storm Emile is now Hurricane Emile, and still picking up steam as it works its way through the Caribbean. It's now projected to be a Category 5 when it makes landfall somewhere in Florida. We're keeping a close eye on it, as evacuation orders are prepped and ready to go if necessary—"

Houseboat switched off the radio. They sat on his boat, still under the cover of night, docked back at Seagull's. Moira had changed, after taking a shower, trying to wash the salt off. A thin film still clung to her, no matter how hard she scrubbed. They had traveled back in silence.

"What did you see?" asked Houseboat, staring at her as they sat in his living room.

"Joan was right," said Moira. "About what she saw.

About what she killed. It was something else. Something pulled from deep below."

"Pulled?"

Moira told him about the ceremony. About Butch. About the obelisk, and the basin, and the salted blood that brought the creature forth. And about it transforming in front of her.

Houseboat stared at her. He took a deep breath and let it out before rubbing his eyes. He looked off, out the window, into the dark. His face betrayed something, something he hadn't said before.

"You've seen something, haven't you?"

"When you were a kid, you always heard those stories about pirates and sailors, right?"

Moira eyed him. *What was he on about?*

"Which ones?" asked Moira.

"The stories about sirens, and mermaids, and other weird things they had seen at sea."

"Sure," said Moira. "Here be dragons."

"Yeah, the great mysteries of sailing out into the unknown. The strange stories sailors would bring back of weird animals and peoples."

"But most of the time it was just a walrus," said Moira.

"Yeah, and racism," said Houseboat. "But sometimes, the stories just didn't make any sense, even with context. And I didn't really understand it until I moved down here. Until I was on the water every day."

"What do you mean?"

"You see things," said Houseboat. "When you're out on the water enough. You ask anyone, and they'll tell you. Strange things, here and there."

"Mermaids?"

"It's never anything like that," said Houseboat. "It's things around the edges. Things you can dismiss. Dark shapes climbing out of the water in your peripheral vision. When you look, they're gone. Stuff missing from your boat. Trinkets, mostly. Things a bird would steal to stick in its nest. Except there aren't any birds an hour out. Little things, around the edges. And the people missing. I don't know. Like I said before, you don't say anything, because saying it makes you crazy. Saying nothing means you're sane."

"Anything that might connect to Butch?"

"Not directly," said Houseboat. "Well—no, it was nothing."

"No, what was it?"

"It was a seagull," said Houseboat.

"A seagull?" asked Moira. "Okay, well, maybe that is nothing."

"It had something in its mouth," said Houseboat. "I was getting gas, in the marina, here. And I wasn't thinking much about anything. Just enjoying the breeze as I filled my boat. And I saw the seagull, not thinking much of it. And then I saw something in its mouth. I tried to pick out what it was, but I couldn't tell. It was something dark, and slimy, and before I could see it, the bird gulped it down. And I didn't think much of it, until it fell off its perch, onto the dock, and—and changed."

"Changed into what?" asked Moira.

"I don't know," said Houseboat. "Something different. Its feathers started falling off, its skin was changing. Its beak was changing. I wanted to get closer, but a part of me said to keep away. Whatever was wrong with it, I didn't want in me."

"What happened to it?"

"It tumbled off into the water," said Houseboat. "And never came back up."

"Did it die?"

"I hope it did," said Houseboat. "But I'm betting what it ate was some of that salt. Something mixed with whatever is in that basin. And it changed it, changed it into something else."

"How many people live on Blackwell Key?" asked Moira.

"Right now?" asked Houseboat. "Five hundred? And that's pushing it."

"And how many people have gone missing over the years?"

"Hundreds," said Houseboat. "And maybe more."

"Have you heard about anyone else missing lately, aside from Bill?" asked Moira.

"No," said Houseboat. "But that's the thing. It's all hearsay, anyway. Joan made a big deal about it, but mostly, people only whisper. Or say nothing at all. And there's been less and less uproar over it as time goes by. You just notice a cashier at the grocery store disappear for a week, and then they're back. Were they really gone? Maybe they took a vacation."

"They were replaced," said Moira. "Replaced with one of those creatures."

Houseboat met her eyes again. He seemed tired, for once. "We're outnumbered, then. It's been decades of it. How many real people are left?"

"I have way more questions than that," said Moira. "What happened to the missing people? What are those things? Why is Butch doing it? Is Butch one of them too?"

"Some of those are easy," said Houseboat.

"Easy?" asked Moira. "None of this is easy."

Houseboat's face had changed. The easygoing Matthew McConaughey vibe was gone. This was the Houseboat who lived in San Francisco, the one who he'd left behind.

"Some of it is," said Houseboat. "The missing people are dead, Moira. Butch lured them out, and he killed them."

Moira sighed. "We don't know that."

"People don't go missing for years unless they want to stay missing, or unless they're dead. They're dead, Moira. Hundreds, dead."

"But why?"

"To control the island," said Houseboat.

"It has to be more than that," said Moira. "And control it how? You're assuming those things serve him, and not the other way around."

HB went silent at that. He shook his head.

"We'll dig ourselves into a hole if we keep talking about it," he said. "Other than what you and Joan saw, we have nothing. We need more info."

"Who do we get it from?" asked Moira. "Those things are the whole island. Hell, maybe even farther out on the Keys."

"We don't know that," said Houseboat. "And that's what I'm saying. We can be suspicious without losing our heads. If everyone was turned, he wouldn't hide anything. He'd keep it out in the open. So it can't be that easy for him, not yet at least. But I don't think we'll get an answer about what those things are, not unless we get it from Butch himself. But the why? The why we can maybe figure out."

"Who can we ask?" asked Moira. "Who's an ally?"

"On the island?" asked Houseboat. "I don't know."

"We could go to the county officials? Or call the feds?" asked Moira.

"And tell them what?" asked Houseboat. "That a substantial portion of Blackwell Key has been replaced by weird creatures? Even if they went to Dagger Key, they'd only find the obelisk. It might be weird, but it's not illegal."

"What about Mike?" asked Moira.

"Mike, who works for Butch?" asked Houseboat. "That seems like playing with fire."

"He led me to you," said Moira. "And to Joan. He's been on the up and up, and not in Butch's pocket."

"But how long until he is?" asked Houseboat. "It'll lead Butch right to us, and then we'll be replaced."

"That is a good question," said Moira. "Why haven't you been targeted?"

"I can't answer that, either," said Houseboat. "Maybe they think I'm harmless. Or maybe I'm not here enough for them to care."

"Or Butch knows he couldn't get you without people noticing," said Moira. "We have to try with Mike. I think we can trust him. And he's close enough to Butch. Maybe he has something else."

"But will he believe us?" asked Houseboat. "Convincing him Butch is some local corrupter is one thing, but convincing him that he's masterminded some sort of alien plot to replace everyone on the island is something else entirely."

"We just gather information?" asked Moira.

"You're a reporter, it's what you do," said Houseboat.

"Yeah, but it seems like we should be doing something," said Moira.

"We're outnumbered and outgunned," said Houseboat. "We have to be smart."

"We don't have time to be smart," said Moira. "Emile is going to be here in five days."

"It may still miss us," said Houseboat.

Images of dark swirling clouds flashed through her mind, images from her visions.

"I saw things," said Moira.

"I know," said Houseboat. "I believe you."

"No," said Moira. "While I was swimming back to you, I had visions. I saw things, mixed with memories. It felt the same as the other night, when I got sick at the potluck. I thought I had just gotten food poisoning, but now—I don't know, I think it's because I got close to them. Being near them made me sick. Made me see things."

"What did you see?"

"I saw those things under the water with me. But, I also saw them at the beginning of time. And I felt something else, something big. Not big. Massive. Just—felt its presence down there, deep down, waiting for something. And I saw a swirling storm."

"A swirling storm?" asked Houseboat. "A hurricane?"

"I don't know," said Moira. "It's hard to parse. My mind was overwhelmed. It was snapshots, intermixed with my memories and—and pain."

"What could the hurricane have to do with anything?" asked Houseboat.

"I don't know," said Moira. "The ritual, the ceremony I saw. It felt like religion. Maybe they worship it."

"That's a big maybe," said Houseboat. "We need to do some research."

"And we need to talk to Mike," said Moira.

Houseboat considered her for a second. "Be smart about it," he said.

"I talk to people for a living," said Moira. "I can handle it."

"I know, I know," said Houseboat. "It's just—maybe I wasn't friends with everyone on Blackwell, but I got along with them. We understood each other. Live and let live, you know?"

"And that illusion has been shattered?"

"Yeah," said Houseboat. "And it's not like anything has drastically changed. It's been like this for a while, I just didn't know about it." He shook his head. "No, that's not it either. I knew about it, or knew enough to be suspicious. But I didn't do anything. I just stood by and watched it happen, all the while thinking things were hunky dory because my life hadn't changed."

"Don't blame yourself," said Moira. "Do you know anyone else you can talk to?"

"You remember Zeb?"

"The burnout from yesterday?"

"Yeah, that's him," said Houseboat.

"He can help us?" asked Moira. "I'd be surprised if he can walk and chew gum at the same time."

"He's smarter than he looks," said Houseboat. "I know, I know, that's not saying much. But he's mentioned before that he has something on Butch. So maybe it's something."

"You said he was messy."

"Oh, he is. But we don't have the luxury of picking and choosing," said Houseboat. "Zeb's got dirty fingers, and sometimes you need dirty fingers."

"I'll trust your judgment. I'll talk to Mike," said Moira. "And see if he's on our side."

14

Moira knocked on Mike's door. The sun had just risen, but the island was still quiet.

Mike answered it blearily, wiping sleep from his eyes, a mug of coffee in hand.

"Moira?" he asked. "Do you ever sleep?"

"I took a nap yesterday," she said. "Mind if I come in?"

"Uh, sure," he said. "Come on in." Mike's house was a small ranch style block home, right in the middle of the north side of the island. She followed him in. "You'll have to forgive the mess. Wait a second—how did you find my address?"

"Land records are public," said Moira. "A five-minute search on my phone."

"Oh," said Mike, his mind still half-asleep. He sat down

at his kitchen table, covered in unopened bills and a couple of newspapers. He gestured to another seat, moving the pile that lay in front of it on the table to the counter.

"Mike—"

He raised a finger, and took a long swallow of coffee, and then one more, then nodded at her to continue.

"We need to talk," said Moira.

"That's what we're doing right now," said Mike. "Not sure why it needed to be at six AM, but I let you in. Want some coffee?"

"No," said Moira. "I've had three energy drinks tonight, I think if I have any more caffeine my brain might shoot out of my head."

"Jesus, that's a lot of caffeine," said Mike. "I never could drink those things. All I taste is chemicals—"

"Mike, please," said Moira.

"Sorry," said Mike. "It's early. My brain hasn't punched in yet."

Moira stared at him.

"Have you noticed anything strange about Butch?"

Mike eyed her. "What do you mean?"

"Anything suspicious? Anything weird?"

"I don't know," said Mike. "I don't think so. He mostly just fishes. If you want some info, you'll have to be more specific. Does this have to do with Joan?"

"Yes," said Moira. "And no. It has to do with everything. Everything on Blackwell Key." Moira tried to read him, but Mike just looked confused and sleepy. "Here. Have you noticed a disproportionate amount of people going missing in Blackwell Key?"

"I mean—" He stopped, paused, and took another

swallow of coffee. "I don't really know what disproportionate is. I don't know what the nationwide average is."

"Florida is on the high side, but six per one hundred thousand," said Moira. "Houseboat tells me Blackwell has one every month."

"That can't be true," said Mike. "I see every missing persons report we get, and Bill is the first we've had this year."

"I'm not talking about official reports," said Moira. "I'm talking about people missing on Blackwell Key. How many don't get reported? How many people disappear for a few days, a week, and then come back, without a report ever getting filed?"

Mike stared at her for a moment longer, blinked, and looked away. "I don't know. There are some, I suppose. Butch generally tells me not to worry about them. Domestic problems, or upset kids. Somebody gets angry, blows up, and goes to live with an uncle or sister for a few days. I mean, I don't think the police should get involved with things like that, at least not when no laws are being broken."

"Do you *know* they go to live with an uncle or a sister for a few days? Or is that just what Butch tells you?"

"Where else would they go?" asked Mike. "They end up back at home. Our population hasn't changed at all. I've lived here four years, and the same faces our always at the community potlucks, at the grocery store, at the marina."

"Why do you think Joan killed Bill?" asked Moira. "A man she loved, with all her heart, and she chopped him up into little pieces in a fit of rage."

"I don't know," said Mike. "She still hasn't talked. Every time we walk in there she looks at us like we're aliens."

"She told me," said Moira.

"She told you?" asked Mike. "Why didn't you tell Butch? It's an active investigation, Moira. You can't withhold evidence—"

"She killed Bill because it *wasn't Bill*," said Moira.

"What the hell is that supposed to mean?" asked Mike. "Butch found him, out on his boat, raving. If it wasn't Bill, who the hell was it?"

Moira told him Joan's story.

"And you believe that?" asked Mike. "That's absolutely insane. Her husband was replaced by some monster? Who just happened to turn back to human *after* she killed him?"

Moira stared at him. His hackles were up.

"Have you ever been to Dagger Key, Mike?" she asked.

"I—no," said Mike. "Why does that matter? It's private property."

Moira remembered Houseboat's words. About trusting Mike.

Fuck it.

"I went there last night," said Moira.

"What? That's trespassing, Moira," said Mike. "I'm a cop! You can't just tell me that."

Moira sighed. "Do you think I'm crazy?" she asked, her voice calm and collected.

"You might be, if you believe Joan, and then sneaked onto Butch's island," said Mike.

Moira told him what she saw, omitting nothing. Mike only stared as she told him the story.

"I—"

"Drink your coffee, Mike," said Moira. Mike pursed his lips and narrowed his eyes, but drank another long swallow.

"Here's what I know," said Moira. "A large percentage of people from Blackwell Key go missing. They disappear for a few days, up to a week. Then, they come back. They come back as something else. The something that comes back is summoned on Dagger Key by Butch. And whatever it is, it isn't human anymore."

Mike took a long breath and then stared into his coffee cup. "I'm out of coffee, and I'm going to need more for this." He got up and filled his mug from the pot. He sat, setting the steaming mug down and squeezing the bridge of his nose before wiping sleep from his eyes.

"That's impossible," said Mike, finally.

"You're right," said Moira. "But I saw it, anyway."

He sighed. "You expect me to believe this."

"I expect you to question it," said Moira. "But you yourself said this is just a job, not a career. That you don't always see eye-to-eye with Butch."

"That doesn't mean I think he's—what did you say—summoning monsters out on his island," said Mike. "That's insane."

"He's killing people," said Moira. "He lures people out of their homes, and then he kills them and replaces them."

"Why would he do that?"

"In service," said Moira. "Service to something else."

"What, like some cult or something?" asked Mike. "But it's not even that. You're saying it works. So it's real, this other force, or something."

"Yes," said Moira. "Are you telling me you've never noticed anything strange on Blackwell Key? You've never seen odd behavior from people here, or from Butch himself?"

"Of course I've seen odd behavior. People are weird, sometimes. But nothing about monsters, or Butch being a cultist."

"Has he mentioned anything about the hurricane lately?"

"What, Emile?" asked Mike. "Jesus, I already forgot. I hope to God it swerves. We can't take a hit from it. It'll wipe us out."

"Has he mentioned it at all?"

"Let me think," said Mike. "I know he's never evacuated from a storm. He brags about it all the time, and he said the same thing this time when the weather report was on, and the word about the governor ordering evacuations. He said this might be the biggest storm Blackwell has ever seen, and he's not going to miss it for the world."

"Does that sound normal to you?" asked Moira.

"No, of course not," said Mike. "But it sounds like a typical Florida Man, and that's not too out there for Butch."

"I saw it," said Moira. "With my own two eyes."

"It was dark," said Mike. "You were hiding in the woods. You could have been seeing things—"

"I didn't make up the thing I saw!" said Moira, raising her voice. "There were no tricks of the light that can explain Butch slipping bloody, salted arms into water, and that thing emerging and changing shape. Have there been any men missing from the island lately, aside from Bill?"

Mike stared at her for a moment. "Don Messina left

his wife a few days ago. Butch told me not to file a report about it. Said Don has a big temper. Probably got a hotel room down in Key West, and he'll be back within a week. He hasn't come back yet."

Moira stared at him, raising her eyebrows.

"It doesn't prove anything," said Mike.

"It proves that you'd rather be quiet than upset the apple cart," said Moira. "What does he look like?"

"Like a dude. Black hair, cut short. Kinda chubby. Early forties. Big nose, no chin."

"That's him!" said Moira. "That's what that thing turned into!"

"What do you want me to do?"

"I want you to help us."

"Help you do what?" asked Mike. "We've got a storm coming, and I'm supposed to what, investigate my boss?"

"He's killing people, one by one, and replacing them."

"Why would he do that?"

"He's preparing for something," said Moira. "I just don't know what."

"It doesn't make any sense," said Mike. "Blackwell is a sleepy little town, full of retirees and beach bums. It's not full of pod people. I thought you were here about climate change."

"I'm a journalist. I follow the story. I don't dictate it."

"I'll keep my eyes open," said Mike. "That's the most I can do right now."

"Make sure he doesn't hurt Joan."

"She's a prisoner."

"He knows she saw something, even if she won't tell him," said Moira. "And he'll try to get her away, to replace her."

"I will not allow a prisoner to be summarily executed," said Mike. "I'm not a monster."

"Can I trust you to keep this conversation private?" asked Moira. "You can't tell Butch."

"What are you planning?" asked Mike. "I can't—"

"We're not planning anything," said Moira. "We're trying to get to the bottom of this."

"Who's we?" asked Mike. He stared at her, and then realized. "Houseboat. Of course. This is all my fault."

Moira sighed. "I've got work to do. Can I trust you?"

"I won't tell him. But I can't keep a secret forever, especially if you keep breaking—"

"Just don't tell him," said Moira. She stood to go. Mike's phone rumbled on the table. "Pretty early for a text."

"Who are you, my mom?" asked Mike. He grabbed his phone and opened the message.

"Well?" asked Moira.

Mike read it, glanced at her, and then back again at the text.

"It's from Butch," he said, finally.

"And?" asked Moira.

"He told me not to worry about Don anymore. That he came back, early this morning."

Moira stared again. Mike met her eyes.

"I'll keep my eyes open."

15

"You need to get the hell out of there," said Martin, his voice tinny over the phone. "That little island is going to be wiped off the Earth, and I don't want you to go down with it."

Moira sat in her room overlooking the ocean as the waves lapped onto the shore beneath her. She'd caught a few hours of sleep, but she was still exhausted, and there was no time to rest. The coming storm had given her a deadline, one that she couldn't put off. She looked to the south, where the storm approached from, but she only saw wispy clouds forming against a clear sky. No sign of the storm that approached. But she knew it was still there, beyond the horizon.

"Martin, it won't be here for days," said Moira. "There's

plenty of time to get out if I need to."

"Every day you wait is another day closer to disaster," said Martin. "There's no use in sticking around in a place that won't exist anymore. Are you going to tell a story about a town that's wiped off the map?"

"There's something happening here," said Moira. "Something happening here with Butch Blackwell."

"What is it?" asked Martin. "It better be good if you're risking your life."

What to tell him?

Martin wouldn't believe what she saw. And if he did, he'd tell her to get out, anyway. That it wasn't worth getting involved in.

"Joan Dermott was the woman who I lined up my first interview with. Her experience is going to color the whole piece. Her missing husband who returned, who she didn't recognize."

"Okay, yes."

"Well, she's in jail here."

"For what?"

"For hacking him to death with an axe," said Moira.

"Christ!"

"Yeah," said Moira. "She told me she saw him transform into some strange creature, and killed it."

"Oh, god," he said. "That's awful."

"But I believe her," said Moira.

"Moira—"

"I don't think she's lying, Martin," said Moira. "And there's a history of missing persons here. I've talked to a local cop, a deputy that works for Butch. He says Butch talks him out of filing reports all the time. Another guy left his wife a week ago and showed up again this morning."

"What does it mean?" asked Martin.

Well, Butch is worshiping some obelisk on his private island, and is summoning void creatures to replace the residents of Blackwell Key. And he's preparing something for the hurricane.

"I don't know," said Moira. "But there's something nefarious happening. He's hiding something, and I intend to find out what it is."

"Promise me you'll get out before it's too late," said Martin.

"I promise," said Moira. "How's your luck?"

"Pretty good so far," said Martin. "The crabbers like me, even if half of them think I'm some socialist prig. I've gotten a lot of good stories about them, and even some acknowledgment about climate change. But there's a lot left to pick out. Funny, since you've mentioned disappearances. One of the crabbers I've been talking to has vanished, along with his boat. Just out of the blue. Very strange."

"Do they know what happened?" asked Moira.

"No," said Martin. "Lit out for the territories. Left his family behind. Makes no sense. Guess I've got my own mystery."

"I guess," said Moira. *What is going on?*

"I'll do my due diligence," said Martin. "Maybe he'll turn up, like your long-lost fella. Let's cross our fingers that's he's not murdered with an axe, though."

"Yeah," said Moira, her voice trailing. "I need to get some research done while the local library is still open."

"Fair enough," said Martin. "Be safe. And don't stick around."

Moira hung up and ate a quick sandwich before heading to the small library right on the edge of the island. As she drove up, a man in overalls was nailing plywood over the front windows of the building, brick with a shingled roof. Moira couldn't tell when it was built, but the bright orange carpet told her it was at least renovated in the seventies or eighties. Moira was slightly surprised to see Sarah from the potluck sitting behind the front counter, shuffling some papers around.

"Oh, hello Moira," she said, smiling widely. "It's nice to see you! Doing some research?"

"Yes, actually," said Moira. The sickness from the potluck instantly came back at the sight of Sarah, the pleasant old lady who had shown her around. She was at the dinner. Was she one of *them*?

All those thoughts flashed through her mind in an instant, but she said nothing, only smiling. "Do you have local newspaper records here?"

"Oh, yes," said Sarah. "Everything on microfiche, in the back room. Do you know how to use the machine?"

"I do," said Moira. "I've used it before."

"Oh, good!" said Sarah. "Everything is back through there." She pointed to a door. "Come and get me if you can't find anything. If we don't have it, it doesn't exist!"

Moira mustered as an authentic smile as she could and turned her back on Sarah, her smile dropping immediately. She needed the information, regardless if she could trust Sarah or not, and she headed to the archive room, heading through the door Sarah had pointed at.

The room was tiny, with a microfiche machine in the corner, and dozens of shelves filled with tiny boxes, boxes

Moira recognized as microfiche storage. She didn't know what she was looking for exactly, but she started by glancing over the boxes. Hoping they were labeled, at least.

Luckily, they were. Moira had gone to small libraries before, where they were shoved into boxes and shelves arbitrarily. Hell, she ended up organizing them more than the librarian ever had. But these were organized neatly in chronological order, and then by newspaper.

The earliest were from the mid-1850s, which Moira hadn't expected. The Keys weren't even connected to the mainland until the early twentieth century, and then only by rail. It wasn't until the 40s that the Seven Mile Bridge was built. Still, Key West was a major city in Florida in the nineteenth century, even without a direct connection to the mainland.

She had a lay of the land. Now she had to figure out what she was looking for.

I need proof of missing people. I need evidence against Butch. And I need to figure out his long-term goals, if any.

She started by looking at papers over the last few years, looking for any mention of Blackwell Key, and its leadership. There wasn't much, with most of the press paying attention to the larger Keys, and Key West in particular, which was the seat of most of the government down there. Whenever Blackwell was mentioned, it was almost always about Butch being re-elected, or some puff piece about some charity event. Indeed, like clockwork, there was a picture of the Blackwell Fish-Off Charity every year, each year a picture buried somewhere in the paper with Butch, the lucky winner for the year, and an enormous fish in between them. Butch's smile was the same as it ever was in those pictures, big, and wide, and gleaming, and dripping with facade.

She went further back, issue by issue, scanning through, looking for any mention of Blackwell. Nothing, nothing, nothing. Charity fish-off, charity fish-off. Re-election.

Now she was twenty years back. How old was Butch? When was he first elected?

And she found the answer soon enough.

Butch Blackwell, son of Ben Blackwell, was elected to police chief, just months after his father's tragic accident at sea. Butch was all smiles at his small celebration event, held at Blackwell Community Center. Ben, long time police chief, had gone out on a routine pleasure cruise and never came back…

"His dad died, and he immediately stepped into his role," said Moira, to herself. She glanced over her shoulder, expecting to find Sarah there, but she still sat alone in the small records room. She found the news report for his disappearance next, repeating the same facts. His age was 43.

She dug back further, looking for anything strange. More Fish-Offs, more elections, Ben Blackwell winning every single one. She was barely looking at the stories now, the same damn picture, almost the same print copy used in every one. Wait, the same picture?

She scanned back, flipping through with the microfiche reader, zooming in on the picture for the charity fish-off. The same layout, with Ben, a big fish, and the winner for the year. This was for 1979, when Butch was just a child. The picture was low resolution, sure, but Ben looked exactly like Butch. The hair style had changed, but the face was the same. That damned smile was the same.

How could that be?

Fathers and sons looked a lot alike frequently, but they weren't twins, for godssakes. Now she was curious, and she went back, but there was no mention of Butch until he won the election for his recently deceased father.

What the hell is going on?

She went further back, seeing the same pattern, over and over again. Did Butch kill his own father, and take over his role?

Moira kept digging, the hours passing as she scanned through hundreds and then thousands of microfiches.

And then she found Ben Blackwell's first election to police chief, a tiny story in the paper. His father, Butch's grandfather, Bo Blackwell had retired abruptly, moving to Maine. Ben's first term as police chief was in 1970. She dug. *When did the fish-off start?*

During Bo's term, it seemed, but those pictures were still featured. And they were the same, with Bo standing there, in place of Ben, in place of Butch. And he looked exactly the fucking same.

This is impossible. Three generations of fathers and sons all looking exactly *the same?*

She studied the picture from 1965. Over fifty years ago, and it might as well have been taken yesterday. They couldn't look the same over three generations. She didn't know the genetic probabilities, but she had to imagine it was near infinitesimal.

Then what was the answer?

It was staring at her in the face, a simple truth, all three men looking exactly the same—*because they were the same*. Butch was Ben who was Bo, and she would bet that if she went back further, she would find more fathers, and more sons, all of them holding positions of power on Blackwell Key. And as she did, she found more names. The lineage of Blackwells back to a news clipping about the settlement of Blackwell Key, by Archibald Blackwell, in the 1870s.

But how? By the same powers that he used to summon those things, and replace the townsfolk with them? How long had he been doing it? He can't have done it the entire time, or the whole town would have been replaced multiple times over. Questions whirled through Moira's mind.

One other piece stood out, the only article she found that focused on a Blackwell, and not the bureaucracy or events of Blackwell Key. It was in the lead up to the Labor Day Hurricane of 1935, which destroyed much of the Keys. There was a minor story about a "storm party" being thrown on Blackwell Key. John Blackwell had invited many of the wealthiest of both South Florida and Key West to attend a party on Blackwell Key, at his estate there.

"We won't get an opportunity like this for decades, most likely," was John's lone quote in the piece. The hurricane would become a Category 5 over the following days and destroy an incredible amount of infrastructure, including the only railroad that connected the lower Keys to the mainland. The article was flippant, written more as a gossip and entertainment piece than anything else. Moira scrubbed through the remainder of the articles, but found no follow up. There were a couple days missing from the time period entirely, presumably everyone too busy not getting killed by a massive storm. Had there been a storm party then? And for what purpose?

She went back to 2017, to Hurricane Irma. Was there any mention of Blackwell Key? Mike had mentioned that Butch had stayed for that.

But there was nothing, at least not on microfiche. She might have more luck online with those.

Moira looked at her phone, and realized it was nearly six o'clock. She'd been in that room for hours. Her stomach rumbled. She'd eaten nothing since early that morning and she had exhausted all the microfiche.

Butch is the only true Blackwell, and he always has been.

A part of her didn't believe it, just like a part of her still screamed inside that this was all impossible. But she had seen it and had the pictures printed out from the microfiche. It still wasn't proof, but it was another piece of circumstantial evidence. But she was sure, more than ever, that Butch was planning something, something big. But who else could she talk to? Where else could she go?

Then it hit her.

The man himself, Butch Blackwell.

16

Butch's house was easy to find. It was the biggest home on Blackwell Key. Still not massive, but new, with easy to spot renovations from when the storm came and tore through the island.

Butch's truck wasn't in the driveway though, off somewhere else. However, a small luxury sedan was parked there.

Butch's wife.

Moira had come intending to talk to Butch again, but maybe his wife was an even better solution. She rang the doorbell.

Something stirred inside, and then footsteps walked to the door, answering it. A blond woman answered, slim, her hair shoulder length, her icy blue eyes sparkling.

"Hello, can I help you?" she asked, her voice light and sweet.

"Hi, I'm Moira Bell, a reporter with public radio," she said, extending a hand. Mrs. Blackwell took it, her skin clammy, and shook it softly.

"Oh, hi," she said. "Butch has mentioned you. You went with him the other day, didn't you?"

"I did," said Moira. "I know I didn't give you any warning, but I was wondering if I could interview you."

"Interview me?" she asked. "Oh—uh, sure. Right now?"

"If possible," said Moira.

"I'm not busy," she said, a slight smile on her face, just as empty as Butch's. "Please come in." She opened the door wider, and Moira followed her, rubbing her fingers free of the salt on the hand that had touched her. The acrid smell of salt filled her nostrils as she entered the house, strong, hitting her like a punch in the nose. She forced herself to follow Butch's wife.

"Is here okay?" she asked, turning to look at Moira, as they stepped into the living room, where a couple of recliners sat opposite a large sectional couch.

"Do you have a dining room?" asked Moira. "I'd prefer that."

"Oh, sure," she replied, and they went farther into the house, really just a ploy by Moira to see more of the place. It looked perfectly normal. A lived-in house, with the normal amount of clutter. The dining room table was nice, and big, with space for eight. A china cabinet stood nearby, and Mrs. Blackwell sat down, gesturing toward an open seat for Moira.

Moira took it and pulled out her phone and notebook.

"Do you mind if I record it?" asked Moira. "So I can go back and check what was said."

"Oh, that's not a problem," said Mrs. Blackwell, though her face told a different story. She wasn't sure of her words.

Moira started recording.

"Can I ask your first name?" asked Moira.

"Oh, I'm sorry," she said. "Betty. Betty Carmichael Blackwell."

"No need to apologize," said Moira. "How are you doing today?"

"I'm alright, I suppose," said Betty. Her eyes kept looking around, focusing on Moira, and then the phone, and then wandered again. "A little worried about that hurricane coming in. But Butch tells me it won't be a big deal."

"Supposed to be a category five when it makes landfall," said Moira.

"Yes," said Betty. "But we've seen bad storms before."

"Who's we?" asked Moira. "You and Butch?"

"Oh, yes," said Betty, with the same vacant smile.

"You mean Irma?" asked Moira. "How did it affect you?"

"It was a close call," said Betty. "It almost hit us."

"I noticed you've had some renovations done on the house," said Moira. "Was that due to Irma?"

"Yes," said Betty. "We had to put in all new floors, replace part of the roof. But like Butch says, it's part of doing business. Cost of living in paradise." Her face changed when she mentioned Butch's name, but Moira couldn't read her. As Moira turned to her notebook, her peripheral vision caught something shifting in Betty, but when she glanced back, it was gone.

A thought entered her mind, one she wanted to dismiss, but couldn't anymore, not after everything she'd seen. And she didn't know what Butch was planning, but even as she entered the Blackwell house, she hadn't considered the possibility.

He wouldn't, would he? Would he replace his own wife with one of those things?

The image of Butch thrusting himself into one of those horrible creatures, its gray flesh softening beneath him, flashed into her mind, and she shuddered.

"You okay, Ms. Bell?" asked Betty. Moira blinked, trying to force the hideous thought out of her mind, but now when she looked to Betty all she saw was those disgusting things, gray sloughing flesh underneath the human skin, smelling of salt and toxic death, hiding in plain sight.

"I'm—I'm fine," said Moira. She forced a smile. "How long have you been with Butch?"

"Oh, it seems like forever," said Betty. Was that sadness Moira heard underneath her voice? Was there still any humanity in there? Was there still a Betty underneath it all, somewhere? Or was it just the chameleon?

"Does it ever feel strange, living on Blackwell Key?" asked Moira.

"What do you mean?"

"I mean, it's your name," said Moira.

"Oh, we don't own it, though," said Betty. "Not anymore, not since the government bought it from us."

"Bought it from you?"

"From the Blackwells," said Betty, correcting herself. She brushed a stray strand of hair out of her face. "I stopped thinking about it, after a while."

"But this place certainly carries Butch's legacy, don't you think?"

"Oh, sure," said Betty. "And he's proud of it. But day-to-day, it doesn't end up mattering much."

"Have you noticed any changes to the island, over the years?"

"Oh, not really," she said. "We've worked really hard to keep the island feeling the same, you know. Like you said, it's part of Butch's legacy."

Moira felt nausea rise in her stomach.

No, not again.

Moira swallowed it down, forced her mind to focus. She wouldn't lose herself again. She wouldn't.

"Have you—have you noticed people missing?" asked Moira.

"Missing?"

"Yes," said Moira. "Locals. Have you ever noticed them going missing?" Moira glanced at Betty, Betty's eyes far away, or maybe deep inside.

"No, I don't think so," said Betty. "I don't think I have. A person would notice something like that."

"Are you sure?" asked Moira. "Betty, have you ever lost a few days?"

"I would remember that, wouldn't I?" asked Betty. "I would remember—" Her face changed again, bunched up in pain, her eyes squinting, and she put a hand to her nose, squeezing the bridge.

"Are you okay?" asked Moira.

"I'm—I'm—" she said, and she squeezed the bridge of her nose hard, and then her face was normal again. "No, I've never gone through anything like that. Just a normal, boring life." She stared at Moira and smiled. The smell of salt rose again, and Moira suddenly felt the revulsion rise, but now it wasn't just nausea, but a sudden rage, the same rage that Joan had described, the rage of being near something so awful, something so inhuman, triggering fight or flight, and Moira would kill Betty, right here, right now, grab a knife from the kitchen and butcher her in the living room—

Then the front door opened and closed, and her mind snapped back to normalcy.

"Honey, who's car—" and Butch stepped into view, towering over both of them.

"Oh, Ms. Bell. Of course," he said. "I didn't realize you had planned an interview with the missus." Moira reached to her phone and slipped it back into her purse, still recording. Butch's smile was there, big, all-encompassing, a grin large enough to swallow her and then the world.

"It was impromptu," said Moira. "Thought I'd pop in while I had the time. If you're free, I'd love to talk to you again."

Butch shook his big head. "Sorry, can't today," he said. "Got a lot of things to take care of." He looked at Betty. "I told Betty the same, but it must have slipped her mind."

"Oh, yes," said Betty, the ragged smile still there. "I had completely forgotten about our plans. I was just trying to be polite."

"No harm in that," said Butch. "But we really should be saying goodbye to Ms. Bell, shouldn't we?" His huge grin hid something else, a deep anger, and Moira sensed it now, the darkness hiding within Butch's wide frame.

"You're right, dear," said Betty. "I'll show her out."

"No need," said Butch. "I'll walk her to the door. You ready, Ms. Bell?"

Butch's question wasn't a question, and Moira grabbed her pen in her hand, gripped it hard, her thumb and forefinger ready to jab the sharp edge into his throat or eye. This was a mistake, a stupid mistake, something she could have done when her piece was still about climate change, and not about whatever dark rituals had taken over Blackwell Key, whatever deep void had settled beneath this place. She shouldn't have come here. She had stepped into the creature's lair, and it was a dark and deadly place, and Butch loomed over her, ready to unhinge his jaw and swallow her whole, feed her to the thing that had replaced his wife.

She betrayed none of those thoughts, only smiling, her pen gripped in her hand, and she stood, walking past a gesturing Butch, who still smiled widely.

"I'd love to chat more with you, Ms. Bell," he said as they walked back to the front door. "But I've got a lot of planning to take care of. County just called, said the governor just put a mandatory evacuation order in place."

"What? Really?" asked Moira.

"Yep," said Butch. "We're going to see a lot of traffic as everybody flies the coop. Emile is coming right for us. It'll be a hell of a thing."

They were at the door now, and Moira went to open it. She felt Butch behind her, her pen still in her hand, ready to defend herself if he attacked her, tried to replace her. But still, he weighed three times as much as she did, and she didn't know if the pen would matter. Was he even human anymore?

As she opened the door a crack, Butch shut it, leaning his palm against it, holding it closed.

"Thought you were writing about climate change, Ms. Bell," he said. "Why do ya gotta interview the missus about climate change?"

Moira turned to face him, and he leaned over her, a foot taller than her. All she smelled was salt, and all she saw was his smile.

"Sometimes things are about more than what they're about," she said. "And sometimes to fully explore a topic, to understand people's beliefs, you have to understand the culture of where they live. So I'm trying to do that."

"Is that why you were digging through the newspaper archives in the library?" asked Butch. He leaned closer to her. "Is that why you're asking about missing folk?"

"I don't know what you're talking about," she said, her voice calm.

"Blackwell Key is a nice place, Ms. Bell," he said. "Full of people who mind their own business, who just want to live their lives."

His breath filled her nostrils, and it smelled of rotten fish and acrid sea water.

"What are you?" she asked, the words spilling out from her, a question she couldn't hold back, no matter how hard she tried.

Butch narrowed his eyes. The smile got wider, and she knew this was it. He would swallow her, and she would disappear forever, into the deep briny void that sat inside him.

"Have you ever drowned, Ms. Bell?" asked Butch, staring at her.

She said nothing, but her face must have betrayed her answer, because Butch nodded, leaning away from her, finally, his rotten breath out of her face again.

"I thought so," he said. "It explains a lot." He took his hand off the door and nodded toward it. "Leave, Ms. Bell. The evacuation order is in effect, and most of the Keys will be headed up to the mainland. I'd suggest you do the same."

17

Moira and Houseboat watched the trail of cars driving north from the deck of his boat. A steady stream of residents had passed through the island over the course of the day. Moira had finally gotten some rest the night before, and came to Houseboat first thing in the morning.

"Those are the smart ones," said Houseboat. "Or at least the smart ones that can leave."

"Are you going to go?" asked Moira.

He glanced at her. "Are you?"

"Butch has no intention of leaving Blackwell Key," said Moira. "So no, I don't think I will."

"What will your buddy up north have to say about that?" asked Houseboat.

"Oh, he'll scream and holler," said Moira. "But he's not

here. He hasn't seen what I've seen."

"If you're staying, I'm staying," said Houseboat. "In for a penny, in for a pound."

"You sure?" asked Moira. She stared at him. "I have a feeling this is going to get a lot worse before it gets better."

Houseboat took a deep breath, and met her eyes. "This is my home. When I said it was the most beautiful place on Earth, I meant it. And I feel—I feel like this is my fault—"

"This isn't—"

"No, no." He waved her off. "I've seen this happen for a long time, and I've never rocked the boat. Maybe I should have." He smiled. "So maybe it's time for me to get up off my ass and do something."

Moira nodded at him. "Well, we do need to do something, but I don't know what," said Moira. "I don't think Butch is one of those creatures. I think he's—something else."

"Something else? Like what?" asked Houseboat.

"I don't know," she said. "But in the newspaper archives, there're photos of him, his father, his grandfather. All look identical. It's not impossible—"

"But damn sure unlikely," said Houseboat. "What you thinking? He's been replacing himself?"

"Something like that," said Moira. "Whenever his persona gets to a certain age, he passes the baton to a younger version."

"And he's been doing that for how long?"

"I imagine as long as there's been Blackwells in the Keys," said Moira. "Maybe even longer. I haven't had the chance to trace the family back, but they claimed the island in the 1870s. Only mention of them I could find any earlier is to a hurricane party, right before the Labor Day Hurricane of 1935, that wiped out a substantial portion of the Keys, and took out the railroad. But he hasn't aged a day in that time."

Houseboat eyed her. "You talk to Mike?"

"Yeah," she said. "I told him the truth."

Houseboat sighed. "I don't know if that's the best course of action—"

"I had to," said Moira. "Claims about Butch being corrupt wouldn't tell the whole story. And he promised that he'd keep his mouth shut and his eyes open. But he wouldn't promise anything more."

"You trust him?"

"Yes," said Moira. "My gut tells me he's our ace in the hole. He's closer to Butch, and might protect Joan if things get dicey. And I think they will as the hurricane draws nearer."

"That storm," said Houseboat. "I don't feel good about it."

"You shouldn't," said Moira. She shook her head. "Have you ever met Betty Blackwell?"

"Butch's wife? No," said Houseboat. "We don't operate in the same circles."

Moira stared at him. "He replaced her. She's one of those things."

"How do you know that?" asked Houseboat.

"I went and talked to her," said Moira.

"Where?"

"His house," said Moira.

"You went to his house," said Houseboat, shaking his head. "Well, you're still here. Can't have gone too bad."

"She's not human," said Moira. "Sometimes, it seemed like her humanity—it kind of peeked through. But I don't know how that makes any sense. If they are truly some awful shapeshifter, a voidborn, like you said—how would they know humanity at all?"

"Maybe they're both," said Houseboat.

"What do you mean?"

"I mean, we don't know what Butch does with the people he replaces," said Houseboat. "We just assumed he killed them and dumped the bodies. But maybe he gives those people to the darkness, to the deep. And they come back that way."

"I don't know," she said. "But his own wife—"

"You said it yourself. He's something else now," said Houseboat. "I don't think he thought twice about it. He's had other wives before this, and he's pulled the same trick with them."

"Fucking Christ," said Moira. "You have any luck with Zeb?"

"About that—"

"Yes?"

"Zeb said he found something. A book. Something old," said Houseboat.

"Okay, great," said Moira. "Do you have it?"

"No," said Houseboat. "I talked to him, but he wouldn't let me have it. Not without seeing you."

"Why?" asked Moira.

"I don't know," said Houseboat, shaking his head. "It's the way he is. He's got to make things harder than they need to be. He's got to make things messy."

"Jesus," said Moira. "Then who cares. We don't need

his book."

"Well, I don't know about that," said Houseboat. "I looked at it. It looks like something that doesn't belong. And where he got it—it's probably worth our time."

"Where did he get it?"

"He told me an estate sale," said Houseboat. "But Zeb doesn't have two sticks to rub together. So I pressed him, and like I figured, he stole it."

"Stole it? Stole it from who?"

"Butch," said Houseboat, smiling now. "Butch bought it at an estate sale, and Zeb stole it."

"How?" asked Moira.

"I didn't ask," said Zeb.

Moira sighed. "Let's talk to him, then. Where is he?"

"He's on the island," said Houseboat. "Not too far. But a fair warning. When I say he makes things messy, I mean it. Zeb will lie until he can't."

"Lovely," said Moira.

*

"I want in," said Zeb. They sat in the living room of Zeb's home. Or at least the house he lived in at the moment. It looked like a grandma's house, with doilies everywhere, and antique furniture, and flower print couches that no one had ever sat on. They sat on them now, and they smelled like mothballs. It's like they had stepped back in time.

Zeb didn't belong here. He wore ratty jeans and a stained tank top, and the faint smell of weed came off him.

"You want in to what?" asked Moira.

"This," said Zeb, gesturing to the two of them, and then himself, and to the huge book that sat on the table near them. Houseboat hadn't lied. It looked like a prop from a movie. Big, thick, leather bound, with ruffled, yellowed pages. No markings on it, except a family crest that Moira didn't recognize. "If you want to read the book, I want to be included in all of this."

"Zeb, you don't even know what we're doing," said Houseboat. "They're evacuating the islands—"

"And yet you guys are staying," said Zeb, his eyes darting between them. "And I know you're trying to fight Butch. Something's going on, and I want in."

"But why?" asked Houseboat.

"Because Butch is an asshole. Because I know something is up on Blackwell. It's always been weird as hell here, and if you know something, I want to be a part of it."

"How do we know the book's important at all?" asked Moira.

"Butch wanted it, so it has to be valuable," said Zeb. "Plus I tried to read it once."

"Tried?" asked Moira. "What happened?"

"I read a page and got a nosebleed," said Zeb. "That thing ain't normal. And I want to know why. You want the book? You have to take me with it."

Moira glanced at Houseboat, and he raised his eyebrows at her in a question. She shrugged.

"Fine," said Moira. She took a deep breath. "Butch is hundreds of years old. In that time, he's slowly replaced nearly the entire population of Blackwell Key, replacing them with shape-shifting fish creatures from a different dimension. He's planning something terrible with the arrival of Hurricane Emile, and we plan on stopping him. We hope that book has the answers."

Zeb stared at her, his face blank, his eyes wide.

"I knew it!" he yelled, suddenly. "That son of a bitch! I knew something was wrong with him. He always hassled me. It explains everything!" Zeb's face was full of confidence and assurance now.

"You're still interested?" asked Moira.

"Of course!" asked Zeb. "I'm in." He pushed the book over to them. "It's yours."

Moira took it in two hands, the massive leather bound tome heavy. She felt something when she held it. Whispers. Echoes.

"Crazy, huh?" asked Zeb. "Let me know what's inside. I'll be ready, for whatever you guys want to do." He paused, and then his eyes went wide. "I know! I can go infiltrate the marina!"

"Don't do that," said Moira. "We're trying to keep a low profile.

"Come on! The best way to gather intel is to be active!" said Zeb, his eyes big.

"We'll call you when we've planned something," said Houseboat. "Don't do anything without telling us."

"Okay, okay," said Zeb. "I'll be ready!"

"We'll be in touch," said Moira, before hurrying out with Houseboat.

*

They were back on Darling, the massive tome sitting on the table in front of Moira. Houseboat sat in his office chair.

"I hope this is worth dealing with Zeb," said Moira.

"I don't plan on talking to him again," said Houseboat. "I told you. He'll only complicate things. By the time he's 'ready', everything will have happened. Hopefully he'll wise up and leave the island." Moira still stared at the book. "Well? What are you waiting for?"

"What?"

"Are you going to read that thing or not?" asked Houseboat.

"I—I'm a little afraid," said Moira.

"I'll read it if you don't want to," said Houseboat. "But fair warning, I'm dyslexic. It'll take me a little longer."

"I can read it," said Moira. "I just need to psyche myself up."

"If something weird happens, I'll be ready," said Houseboat.

"What could happen?" asked Moira. "Now you're scaring me more."

"I don't know," said Houseboat. "But after everything that's already happened, I'm prepared for anything."

"Well, here goes nothing," said Moira.

She opened the book.

18

January 1st, 1935.

John Blackwell has recommended that I start my own tome, in pattern after his, and I took his advice. He suggested a large book. I dismissed it as nonsense at first. Why would I need something so large? But then he told me that the size mattered. The book would contain horrible knowledge, knowledge not meant for human language, for human words. And it would strain at those words, and would strain at the paper, and would strain at the book. The larger you made each, he said, the longer it would hold. And so I sent for this from New York. Special construction that took a month to get here, but here it is.

Blackwell says to plan for this year. The void has called

to him, and told him that the next season will be the one. And he has made allusions before, but never specific, and so I trust him. I trust that this will be the year, and we will finally prove successful.

January 31st, 1935.

We've erected a new monolith. It is something to be seen. It dwarfs the old one, the one we have relied on for years. It is partially the reason Blackwell is so confident in this year. He truly believes that with it we will find success. And after seeing it, it is hard to argue. He contracted it in secret, from a sculptor overseas. It arrived here on confidential manifest, and only the artist himself had seen it before we set eyes on it, and set it in place of the old monolith, the one Blackwell's grandfather had installed, generations ago. As we unpacked it, Blackwell told us news of the sculptor. He had carved the shape as instructed, and then packed and shipped it to us, per Blackwell's direction. Before it arrived, news arrived of the artist.

He killed himself. Filled his bathtub, after dinner with his family. And then drowned himself in it.

We christen it tonight.

February 1st, 1935.

My heart still beats like a drum from last night. My blood runs hot. It is impossible not to, not after what I saw, not after what we accomplished. We christened the obelisk, out on

Dagger Key. Me, Blackwell, Sharp, and Thornton. The four of us, we plunged knives into our arms, and then rubbed it with salt. The pain almost sent me into unconsciousness, but I forced myself to stay awake, and then we fed the shape with our blood.

And it blossomed. The void reached out from its base, filling the basin, filling the basin with its darkness. And Blackwell is right. This will do it. It has to. The void, I could smell it, and I could feel it. And Blackwell told us to sink our bleeding arms into it.

I didn't, not at first. I hesitated. But then he showed us, plunging them into the void, and they came back clean. And we all followed suit.

We all were healed by its power. And I could hear it. I could hear it speak.

Down below, it called to me.

March 24th, 1935.

We have spoken to the void as often as we can, doing the rituals, over and over again, our wounds bled and then cleaned, over and over again. We feed the void with our pain, with our salt, and it rewards us with knowledge.

But it wants more. It wants more than just blood. It wants life. And after our ritual, Blackwell insisted we must escalate. We must give it what it wants if we are to finish this year.

All of us balked at first, aside from Blackwell. No one considered the cost. No one thought that it would ask for more. Blackwell knew. Blackwell knew all along.

He convinced the three of us. He said he would pay it

first, to show his dedication and his faith.
Tonight, we deliver his beloved to the void.

March 25th, 1935.

She screamed as it took her.

March 29th, 1935.

Something came out of the void. A thing, a servant of The One Who Sleeps. And it became Blackwell's wife. Identical. She behaved and spoke the same, and Blackwell treats her as if she is the same.
But that thing is not Laura. It may look and act like her, but I know it is not her. Nothing will convince me otherwise.
The One has not been satiated. We must continue.
My Addison will be given next.
I gave my word. My faith will be proven.

May 16th, 1935.

The children have stopped asking questions about the disappearance and reappearance of their mother.

Blackwell tells us the children will be next.

It will be worth the sacrifice.

June 20th, 1935.

I am struggling to continue. We have replaced all of

our immediate family with the shapeshifters, and several of our close business contacts as well. Perhaps Blackwell is telling the truth when he finds the company of those things better than humanity, but I cannot. I cannot silo away the knowledge of what they truly are underneath, and despite my lies, I suspect Blackwell knows. Still, his behavior toward me, and the others, has largely gone unchanged. He is more enthusiastic than ever about our opportunity this year. He says we will finally awaken The One. It is only a matter of faith.

August 25th, 1935.

We have fed the void, over and over and over again. I find it difficult to sleep at night now, with those things in my house. I am not sure they sleep.

But the storm approaches, and Blackwell says this will be the one. That the seas have finally warmed enough for the long frozen One to awaken. To transform the Earth, to bring it back to its natural state. He promises us an eternity in a new paradise, with us as kings upon the Earth.

I do not believe him, not anymore. Not after looking into the eyes of what Addison has become. She cannot smile like she once did. It is only performance.

But still, I will perform the ritual on the night of the storm's arrival. If it awakens the One, and the void spreads, so be it. I have nothing else left.

September 1st, 1935.

We performed the ritual, as the storm howled around us.

What Dwells Beneath The Waves

I have never born witness to a calamity so great. The winds threatened to knock us over, to rip the very water from the sea, but Blackwell was a man possessed, pushing us toward the obelisk, even as our boat capsized. We swam through dark waters that tried to pull us under.

It was worth the cost. That is all he said. And the storm approached us, and we performed the ritual. Again, and again, feeding the void with our salted blood, the torrent of pain, reaching down into the darkness.

And Blackwell told us to stop, that it was time, and he spoke what he was told to speak. The language we all know, the language that bursts at our throat and lungs, and leaves us with scorched tongues and burnt mouths every time we utter it. Indeed, fire came from between his lips, fire and salt, but Blackwell only continued.

But nothing happened. He spoke for hours, and the storm swirled around us, and then weakened. We heard the Beast, and felt it, and we waited for the One That Dwells Beneath The Waves to rise from the depths.

It did not happen.

Blackwell still waited on Dagger Key, hours after the storm passed. We three returned to our families, or what passed for them.

This will be my last journal entry, and I do not intend to live with the guilt I've piled upon myself. I oiled and tested the revolver yesterday.

It fires.

*

"Jesus Christ," said Moira, shaking her head.

Houseboat started awake. He'd been napping in his chair, his head leaned forward.

"What time is it?" asked Moira.

"Five," said Houseboat, looking at his watch. "You've been nose deep in that thing for hours."

"I was lost in it," said Moira.

"What does it say?" asked Houseboat.

"It says a lot," said Moira. Moira told him what she read.

"Fucking hell," said Houseboat.

"I've felt it," said Moira.

"Felt what?"

"The One That Dwells Beneath the Waves," said Moira. "When I drowned. In the visions I've had here. I was down in the water, dying. Water in my lungs. But I wasn't alone. It was some great, terrible thing, down deep, so far down that no one would ever see it. And I felt it."

"But it didn't work," said Houseboat. "They failed. Obviously."

"Yes," said Moira. "Because the men *didn't* have faith. They didn't believe. But Butch does believe, and he's the only one left. The only human left. And I don't think he intends to fail with this storm."

19

She needed to know. She needed to know how bad it truly was, and so Moira went to the community potluck again, the second week in a row.

Cars still streamed by on US-1, heading back toward the mainland, but the traffic had slowed over the days, as less and less people remained. The hurricane was only two days away.

But you couldn't tell that by the parking lot at the community center. It was full, and as Moira approached, the buzzing sound of residents talking filtered outside. Houseboat told her not to go. That it was too late. But she had to talk sense into some of them. Some of them still had to be human, some of them could be saved.

Moira knew it was a mistake as soon as she stepped inside. The same people were there as the previous week, all at their familiar places, a long table full of casseroles there again. The same two punch bowls, filled with the same punch. Sarah, the librarian, came over and grabbed Moira by the arm. Moira couldn't spot Butch as they walked to the same table.

"You came back!" she said, her voice full of glee, but Moira only pictured whatever lurked beneath the skin of the kindly old lady, the gray, sallow, soft flesh of the void. Sarah walked her back to their table, a chair for her ready. The same seat as before, and everyone around the table all smiled and said hello, and they all remembered her name.

But Moira felt the darkness in the room, felt the grasp of the deep pulling at her from every direction. She had dismissed the feeling before, before she knew, before she had seen what Butch did on Dagger Key, before she had read the cost of summoning these things. Sarah spoke to her and Moira looked in her kindly face, imagining Butch and his deputies dragging her to the pit, and the cold grasp of the deep pulling her below, and a few days later, this *thing* emerging, being both Sarah and not, a twisted amalgamation of what that creature thought Sarah was.

"Dear? How has Blackwell been treating you?" asked Sarah.

"Oh, sorry, I was in another world," said Moira, trying to smile, but knowing it came off as insincere.

"That happens," said Sarah. "You lose yourself here." Sarah smiled.

"It's treating me fine," said Moira, lying through her teeth. "I'm just worried about the big storm coming. Isn't there a mandatory evacuation?"

"Oh, that doesn't mean anything," said Sarah. "They said that about Irma too, and I stayed put, and everything worked out fine." And in sequence, the rest of the table echoed her sentiments, all the older ladies each spouting off the same facts, about how it was perfectly safe, and how they were conchs, and a little wind and rain wouldn't scare them away.

— *If it floods, we'll go to the roof —*

— *My insurance covers everything —*

— *We welcome the rising tide, the warming waters —*

And Moira looked to who said what, but the clashing voices overwhelmed her, and she could only smile, and then closed her eyes. Sarah's hand still lay on her shoulder. She had to get up, she needed out.

"I'm going to get a drink," she said. "I'll be right back."

"Can't wait, dear," said Sarah, that same slim smile on her face, the thin lips of the older woman painted dark red.

Moira pushed away from the table, away from the hand of Sarah and the identical faces of the women, and she immediately felt better, like she could breathe again, even if she was still surrounded. She went to the long table, covered in a tablecloth adorned with pineapples. The casseroles were there, different from last time but the same, and she stared at them all. Were they poison? Could these things eat food at all? She remembered Joan's story of her not-husband downing a bucket of briny sludge in the backyard, and the thought made her stomach turn.

The two punch bowls were filled with red and orange liquid, but she couldn't trust either. Instead, Moira grabbed a cup and walked to the bathroom, locking the door behind her, and filling it from the tap. She sipped at the cool water and felt better.

She stepped out of the bathroom, and took two steps before coming face to face with Don Messina, the man who recently returned.

The man she saw rise out of the void. Summoned by Butch and his deputies.

The sight of him froze Moira.

"You okay, Ms. Bell?" he asked. He wore jeans and a polo shirt, holding a cup. Dressed normally, looking normal, but she knew it lurked underneath.

"I—I don't think we've met," said Moira.

"Oh, I'm sorry," he said. He extended his free hand. "I'm Don. Butch told me all about you."

Moira wanted to scream at him. She wanted to chop him up into little pieces, like Joan had done, sudden inexplicable rage filling her.

But she shook his hand, even as touching him made her feel sick to her stomach. It felt normal, his hand warm and his skin soft, but she knew that hiding behind it was sallow, gray flesh that would meld and merge and change into whatever the void was fed.

"Oh," she said. "Hello. Nice to meet you." She knew she should talk to him, try to get more info from him, but every atom of her body told her to get away, to escape from whatever thing he was, whatever thing that all these people were.

Because she knew now, she knew that there was no one worth saving here, not at the potluck at least. They all served Butch, because he had replaced them all. She glanced around the room and saw all of them talking, all of them babbling back and forth, their lives the same every day, their minds both human and alien. She didn't know how they worked, or how much humanity was left, but she knew now they couldn't be saved. They couldn't be pulled back in from the void. Whatever the void took, whatever it fed upon, it couldn't be healed, or built back up. They were irretrievable.

Houseboat was right. This was a mistake.

She needed to get out of there. Let them all drown.

"Moira," said Mike, appearing out of nowhere. "What are you doing here?"

"I—I thought I could talk some people out of staying," said Moira. "I—I can't stay here. I need to get some air."

"Here," said Mike, and he ushered her out through a side door. The crisp night air felt fresh again, and Moira rubbed her face, taking deep breaths.

"You feel alright?" asked Mike.

"No," said Moira. "I thought I could talk some sense into them—"

"It's not going to happen," said Mike. "Everyone here are the diehards, Moira. You've got good intentions, but you can't save everyone. If I were you, I'd get out of here."

"Have you noticed anything?" asked Moira. "Have you seen anything strange?"

"No," said Mike. "I've kept my eyes open, but I haven't seen anything out of the ordinary."

"What about Joan?"

"She's in her cell."

"I've got things to show you," said Moira. "Evidence."

"Real evidence?" asked Mike.

"Yes," said Moira. "It's with Houseboat—"

A big hand clamped down on each of their shoulders, and Butch stood there, a big grin on his face.

"I see you two are getting along," said Butch.

"Ms. Bell was feeling ill," said Mike. "I was making sure she was alright."

"That's awful kind of you," said Butch. "You're a good one, Mike. Don't let anyone tell you different. But I think Sawyer needs you inside. Said he needs your help with something."

"Right now?" asked Mike, his eyes narrowed.

"You better hurry," said Butch. "He was acting like it was an emergency." Butch smiled even wider. "Go on now. I'll look after Ms. Bell."

Mike went inside, with a glance back at Moira.

"Get your hand off of me," said Moira, but Butch only clamped down harder, and she tried to pull away, but couldn't. Butch leaned in close.

"These people don't need saving from you," said Butch. "It's always been the way. Always somebody from up north, thinking they know better. Thinking that they can save us from ourselves. You just let us be, Ms. Bell. That storm is coming through, and your kind aren't prepared for the destruction it will cause."

"My kind," said Moira. "You mean humans. You mean whatever you used to be."

"Now, now," said Butch. "I said nothing of the like. You said that. Reporters always putting words in people's mouths. And you wonder why nobody trusts you. All you do is twist other people around into a pretzel."

"Let go of me," she said again, struggling, but his grip was like iron, even as he didn't seem to be trying at all.

"I don't know what you've dug up, Ms. Bell, but I think it's best if you left it all alone. Put it back where you found it and forget it ever existed. Catch and release, you know."

"I know what you're doing," said Moira. "I know what you are."

Butch laughed at that, even as his grip squeezed even tighter on her shoulder. She gritted her teeth.

"You have no idea," said Butch. "You're lucky, you know. I already got attention on me from the county because I'm not evacuating. Normally, if someone came into my home, disturbing my wife, I wouldn't be so kind."

"She's not your wife," said Moira. "If she was, she's certainly not now. She's one of those *things*."

Butch's facade collapsed, the large, uncanny smile disappearing, his face naked without it. Dark.

He sighed, an empty noise.

"This is my last warning," he said, and then he took a deep breath, and exhaled on her, warm air laden with salt covering her face, and then she coughed, and she fell into darkness.

20

It's worse this time.

Moira is a child again, playing in the cool water of the Atlantic, her parents up on the shore, not seeing her disappear deeper and deeper. They don't see the riptide pulling her away.

But it's not water. The dark liquid rose around her, pulling at her, but it wasn't water. It was viscous, clinging to her, black. She had thought it was tar, when she had seen it, but tar was from this Earth, something recognizable, something germane.

This was alien, something from somewhere so deep and dark they've never seen it, and any who has have changed too much to call human anymore. Dark, and salted, and depthless, as her feet tried to touch bottom, to find purchase, but there was nothing.

So she pushed to the surface, to escape with a breath, and swim back to her parents, but her parents were gone, the beach deserted, the landscape changed. The sky had darkened now, raining the filth that filled the oceans. The clouds of darkened sludge covered the sky, and all the land was blemished by the changes.

Moira looked for help, looked for anyone to shout to, to pull her from this hellish pool, but there was no one, the land deserted.

No.

That wasn't true.

They were there, innumerable, legion, a horde of them, pulled from the muck and the mire, pulled, summoned by their leader, and pushed out into the world, to change it to something more suitable. To march across the land with sallow, soft flesh, and to absorb anything and everything, and make the world their own, to make this land like theirs. Their chests heaved with forced breaths, the air still alien to them, harsh on their systems. But soon the air would change, and be filled with enough salt and death to soothe their breath.

And the Servants of the Deep crossed the land, wherever water met land, and they crossed over, and they absorbed. Any human it touched became part of the deep, and no matter the violence, the guns, the knives, the explosives, they could not be stopped. Because there was no limit to them. Their master had awoken, and with it, they were invincible, impossible, unending.

The Servants were not alone. As Moira looked out over the Earth, and she saw it all, all in her mind's eye, there was nothing she couldn't see. The Touch of the Deep made her see it all.

So she could see the Servants' companions, the lieutenants that led them through the land.

Moira recognized their face, recognized their *smile*. She had seen it on the face of Butch, and those were the men who led these creatures across the Earth, showing them the soft spots where they could feed and swallow and absorb the life of the Earth. They strode alongside them, confident in their hatred, in their faith, in the face of death and torture of their own, and they smiled, and they lined up for their new master, and bowed as it approached, their smiles wider still, their jaws cracking as they reared back to choke down what it fed them. They choked down the dark brine, filling them until they burst, and they beamed, happy with their deeds.

Smiling men, with melting faces, they looked up to see their master as he strode upon the Earth.

Looming over everything is a great shape, holding court. It observes. It watches. It tallies all, an intelligence indescribable. It looks down upon this Earth and recognizes nothing of us, nothing but raw resource, ready to be harvested. It strode this land long ago, back before time had memory, before God was born, when the land was kinder to its biology, but then it changed, and it was sentenced to the deep, its kin and Servants bound to the darkness, to the dark void that lurked between cracks and shadows.

It slept, it slept, it slept, with an eye cracked, mustering the energy to observe for a moment, over eons, to see if it was safe, to search for new harbingers, new men who it could bend to serve. Bend them with promises of paradise and fortune and anything they wanted, but all they would get is the void, filling them to the brim, and then overflowing, coating their innards with darkness. It would drive them to sacrifice everything they ever knew or cared for, would eat their empathy, and take these leaders of men, and encourage them to start wars, and kill their land. Drive off heroes, and cut them down before they could begin. To do whatever was necessary to prepare for its arrival.

And now it had arrived, lurching out of the depths of the darkest oceans, ripping open the seams between the void and the ocean depths, the water warm enough to weaken the threshold. Awaking and pulling itself through, pushing itself to its feet, where it strode, stepping out of the vast ocean to rule once again. The land had been prepared, and now there was no stopping it.

It moved. With great movement, it covered hundreds of miles with a single stride, leaving lakes of toxic darkness behind with every step, converting the ground itself into a polluted wasteland. It strode over man and beast alike, and they all died, burning in its shadow, unable to exist alongside such a thing. Its alien existence burned at their biology, their cell walls collapsing in its presence.

Anything that didn't burn away wept at the sight of it, the size and scope something unheard of, something that a film couldn't communicate. The minds of those who saw it ripped at the seams, bursting from within. The people wept at its approach, falling to their knees, unable to understand what the great thing was, only knowing that it was their end, the end of them, the end of humanity. They wept, and they tore at their skin, and wailed a terrible sound.

And the dark liquid pulled Moira under, and it filled her lungs, and the Servants pulled her under, pulled her down to the ocean floor, where they would keep her forever. No future, no present, no past, just the void, just the darkness, and she would stay there, slowly being consumed by it until there was nothing left of her.

No

Not like this

She struggled in their grasp, and they did not understand. Once in the void, there was no struggle, there was nothing but compliance, no resistance, never, the oppression drove it from you.

But Moira fought them, the little girl she was. Her tiny frame punched and kicked, and their soft flesh gave way, and she got free, and floated back to the surface.

Her father pulled her from the surf, and carried her to the wet sand, the beach filling now, a lifeguard running toward them, her mother screaming for help. The guard pounded on her chest, and she woke, coughing up water.

Just water.

21

Moira heard water lapping and she jolted up, her hands splayed out, grabbing for anything, the feeling of sludge in her lungs still present, right on top, and she gasped for breath.

"You're okay," said Mike. Moira stared at him, unable to recognize him, unable to recognize anything.

"The Thing, it sleeps, the Great Beast, but soon it will march across the land, and its emissaries will absorb them, the smiling lieutenants will unhinge their jaws—"

"Moira!" said Houseboat, coming in from outside. "You're on my boat. You're not making any sense."

"I felt it, I felt it. Underneath the waves, it waits, where the fabric is thinnest, deep in the dark—"

The words tumbled out of her, out of her control, but

she saw Mike, and Houseboat, and knew them, and saw she was in the dimly lit interior of the boat, now familiar to her. Her heart raced inside her chest, but she forced herself to take a deep breath, and stem the flow of the tide of words that poured from her throat.

"I—I," she said, forcing her tongue to slow. "I—what happened?"

"I left you outside with Butch," said Mike. "I shouldn't have left, but I didn't think—I didn't think he would do anything, not in public. I found you stumbling along the highway. You were gone."

"Butch," said Moira. She blinked, and breathed, and the words came now, her own words. "Butch said this was my final warning. He breathed onto me, and I—"

"And you what?" asked Houseboat.

"I went somewhere else," said Moira. "I remember it, now. I'd been there before, after the potluck, the first time. Memories of my childhood, and dark figures, under the water. But I remember."

"Remember what?" asked Mike.

"What I saw," said Moira. "I saw what Butch wants. He wants to transform the Earth."

"But why?"

"Because he serves It. A great slumbering creature, that sleeps at the bottom of the sea, at the threshold between worlds." She didn't have to think to explain it that way. She just knew those words and their meaning.

"I don't—" said Mike, rubbing his face and walking away. He came back. "Butch is a sport fisherman. He wears trucker hats. Jesus Christ, I had to explain what algebra was to him the other day."

"A wolf in sheep's clothing," said Houseboat.

"How do you feel?" asked Mike.

"I'm okay, now," said Moira. "Butch said he had too much attention on him from the hubbub about the evacuation orders. So that's probably why he only did whatever he did, and not black-bag me. But I feel okay. Feel like I could sleep for a year."

"Black-bag you?" asked Mike.

"Are you still not convinced?" asked Moira.

"Do I think Butch is up to some shady shit? Yes, undoubtedly," said Mike. "But worshiping some cult god? It's absurd!"

Moira looked to Houseboat. "You didn't show him?"

"Show me what?" asked Mike.

"I was waiting on you," said Houseboat.

"Why? Do you think two crazy-sounding people are better than one?"

"Well—yes," said Houseboat. "Strength in numbers."

"Show me what?" asked Mike. "What the hell are you two talking about?"

"Show him the book," said Moira. "Let him read it. And the pictures, from the old newspapers."

Houseboat nodded and went to his safe.

"What book?" asked Mike.

"A journal from the old Keys," said Moira. "An associate of Butch's, in 1935." Houseboat opened the safe and pulled out the book, and the file folder with the printings from the newspapers Moira had found. He set them down on the desk with a thud.

"Jesus," said Mike. "What do you mean, associate of Butch? Butch was born in the late 70s."

"No, he wasn't," said Moira. She pointed at the newspaper clippings. "Three generations, all looking exactly the same. The elder Blackwell disappearing as soon as it's convenient."

"Family resemblances are a thing," he said. He studied the pictures closely. "But Jesus, they do look *exactly* the same. What does the journal say?"

"You should read it for yourself," said Houseboat.

"Do I have to?" asked Mike. "I'll believe you. Tell me what's in it."

"An associate of John Blackwell, an alias of Butch, wrote it, in 1935, leading up to the Labor Day Hurricane which devastated the Keys. He details the same thing happening back then. Butch and a few other men replaced members of their families with some sort of creature, and then performed a ritual on the storm, trying to summon a dark god from below the water."

Mike took a deep breath and scratched at his scalp. "Well, it clearly didn't work."

"No, it didn't," said Moira. "The man who wrote this killed and replaced his family, and then committed suicide when the final ritual failed. And I checked the records. It confirms his suicide, only after he killed his wife and children."

"And you're saying Butch has made himself immortal and is trying to do the same thing again?"

"Yes," said Moira. "And most of the population of Blackwell Key is something else now. Those creatures, summoned from the void, out on Dagger Key."

"Christ," said Mike. "I'm struggling. You know all this for sure?"

"After what I saw tonight, yes," said Moira. "I don't know all the details, but they don't matter. Butch intends to wake that thing, and bring it back to Earth."

"Bring it back?" asked Houseboat.

"Yes," said Moira. "It was here before, before man, before life. It came here back then, back when the Earth was closer to what it was used to. And then it cooled down, and it retreated to the bottom of the ocean to sleep. Until someone could wake it up."

"What is it, exactly?" asked Mike. "Just some big monster? Like Godzilla?"

"No," said Moira. "I don't think so. It's something else. You ever read Lovecraft?"

"I—I don't read much," said Mike.

"Jesus Christ," said Moira. "I don't think bombs or missiles will hurt this thing. It doesn't work like us. This is the end of the world. This is apocalypse. It will make the Earth unlivable. It will kill us all. It won't only kill humanity. It will kill life."

"I need a drink," said Mike. Houseboat shrugged and reached underneath his desk, pulling out a bottle of Jack Daniels.

"Thanks, but that's probably a bad idea right now, no matter how much I want it," said Mike. "Butch is trying to end the world."

"You need to stop thinking about him like he's human," said Moira.

"Is he one of those things?" asked Houseboat.

"No," said Moira. "I think his deputies are. But Butch also isn't human anymore. He stopped a long time ago. Or maybe he lost it over the years. It slipped out of him, little by little, and now there's none left. But whatever you think of as Butch is mimicry. It's performance. What's underneath, he only lets slip out when he's caught off guard. I saw it for a moment when I fished with him, when I first met him. I saw it again earlier tonight, for longer. He's not some bumpkin. He knows what he's doing, and he's been planning this for a *long* time."

"He invited me out to Dagger Key," said Mike. "Couple months ago. I couldn't go. Too busy. He kept saying he was going to invite me back. He would have changed me, wouldn't he? Into one of those things?"

"I think it's the other way around," said Moira. "He changes those things into you."

They all fell silent.

Mike's eyes were somewhere else, and his hands went to his face.

"I'm sorry, I need a minute," he said, and he left, walking out onto the dock. Moira looked at Houseboat, who sat down, and took a slug from the bottle of Jack.

Moira followed Mike outside. He was sitting at the end of the dock, staring out into the darkness. She walked up behind him.

"I helped him, Moira," said Mike, his voice empty.

"I don't think that's true," said Moira. "I don't think you helped kidnap any people and turn them into—into whatever those things are."

"I looked the other way," said Mike. "Even when my gut said otherwise. And I don't want to believe it."

"It's difficult to wrap your head around."

"I don't *want* to believe it. Because that means I sat back and let little old ladies get taken by whatever he is.

All I can think about it is how many times I let it slide. All because Butch told me it was normal. I was—I was just following orders."

Moira stood silent behind him.

"Give me a few minutes," he said. "I'll be inside."

Moira thought to say something else, but instead left him, going back in. Houseboat had stowed the booze again. He raised an eyebrow at Moira.

"He'll be back inside shortly," she said. "He feels guilty."

Houseboat eyed her. "He's not the only one."

Within a minute Mike was back inside. He looked at both of them. "I want to help. What do we do?" asked Mike, breaking the silence.

"We stop Butch," said Moira.

"How?" asked Houseboat.

"We interrupt the ceremony," said Moira. "Or we kill him."

"You just said he's lived over a hundred years," said Mike. "Can he even die?"

"I don't know," said Moira. "But we have to stop him."

"Emile will make landfall tomorrow night," said Mike. "It's going to be hell here. Winds over 150 miles per hour. Storm surge and flooding might cover the entire island. There won't be anyone to help us if we get fucked. Anyone left down here will be hunkered down."

"That's our advantage," said Moira.

"Like hell it is," said Mike. "I've been out in a hurricane, and it's a nightmare. I can't imagine it down here."

"This boat can take it," said Houseboat.

"You say that," said Mike. "Until a stray 200 MPH wind capsizes it with us aboard in open water. It'll kill us."

"I've made some alterations to Darling over the years," said Houseboat. "She can take it. Or as well as any other boat this size can."

"Butch will be ready for us," said Moira.

"And there's only three of us," said Mike. "He's got an entire island of servants, if those things do follow his orders."

"There's four of us," said Moira.

"Who's number four?" asked Mike.

"Joan," said Moira.

"She's in a cell," said Mike. "She's not helping anyone right now."

"If we leave her in there, she's as good as dead. Is the Blackwell Police Station flood-proof?"

"No," said Mike. "Hell, we get some water in the front even when it rains a little."

"And I doubt Butch plans to move her someplace else," said Moira. "We need to get her out."

"Jailbreak?" asked Houseboat.

"Yes," said Moira. "It'll give us another ally, and every extra set of hands is vital. And I can't just leave her there to die."

"You won't hear an argument from me," said Houseboat. They looked at Mike.

"Can you get us in?" asked Moira.

"My next shift isn't until tomorrow night," said Mike. "Can we wait until then?"

"Will you be alone at the station?" asked Moira.

"Yes," said Mike.

"Then it's perfect," she said. "We break out Joan, we take weapons from the station, and then we head to Dagger Key, before the worst of the storm hits. We destroy the obelisk, and that's all she wrote."

"You make it sound so easy," said Mike.

"What is that obelisk made from?" asked Houseboat.

"I don't know," said Moira. "It's black. Could be obsidian. Could be iron."

"That makes a big difference," said Houseboat.

"I saw it from a distance, at night, in torchlight," said Moira. "It's the best I can do."

"Well," said Houseboat. "I'll prepare for iron, and if it's only obsidian, then we'll have to accept a few degrees of overkill."

"Overkill with what?" asked Mike.

Houseboat stared at him, confused. "How do you expect us to take down some massive piece of stone? With picks and shovels?"

"I hadn't thought that far in advance," said Mike. "Until an hour ago, I thought both of you were insane."

"Well, I have thought that far in advance," said Houseboat. "We need a bomb."

"Oh, well, I'll just drive down to the bomb store," said Mike.

"You don't have to be a smart-ass," said Houseboat. "I'll make us one. A day is plenty of time."

Mike stared for a second. "Of course. I should have guessed."

Moira looked to Houseboat. "Can you make something strong enough to break iron?"

"Yeah," said Houseboat. "We might want to be clear of it, though."

"Well, if it's the end of the world otherwise, we'll find a

way," said Moira.

"So, tomorrow night?" asked Mike. "What should I do in the meantime?"

"Lay low and get some rest," said Moira. "Do you have any guns, aside from your service pistol?"

"I've got a shotgun," said Mike. "But that's it."

"Well, get it ready," said Moira. "We're going to need it. What time does your shift start?"

"6 PM," said Mike.

"I'll be there at 6:30," said Moira.

"The rain will be heavy by then," said Mike. "Be ready."

"I've been in storms before," said Moira.

"Not a Florida hurricane, though," said Mike. "Not down here."

Rain started tapping on the roof of the boat, a light sprinkle.

22

The rain grew and grew throughout the night, and into the next day as Emile approached. Moira slept through the night, the waves crashing below at her at the Blue Dolphin, the rain tapping harder and harder against the roof as she slept.

She woke up early. Bea smoked a cigarette underneath an overhang at the main office. Moira waved at her, but doubted that Bea was there at all. She was probably a Servant. Bea was incredulous that Moira was staying through the storm.

The cars passing through came few and far between now, the last stragglers out before the hurricane arrived in full force. The water already was a few inches deep in some places. It would only get deeper.

She tried to contact Martin through text and phone, but he didn't answer either. It wasn't like him, but he might just be neck deep in a story, and didn't have the time. She understood it. Still, she needed to tell him what was happening, even if he didn't believe her.

Moira recognized she might not make it out alive tonight, and if she died, the story needed to get out of there, in some form or the other.

Unless he wakes the Beast, and then you won't need a story. It will be awake, and it will transform the Earth—

She cut off the idea in her mind. They would stop Butch.

She used her phone to scan everything, the photos, the old newspaper articles, and even the pages of the old diary. Everything that pointed to the conspiracy, and then added her notes from her interviews with Joan, her firsthand experience. Everything, even the stuff that was impossible to prove, like her visions. She uploaded them to the cloud, with multiple fail-safes, and then emailed them to Martin, and to their group editor, Joe. Joe would probably think she was crazy, but she had to get it up while she still had internet and service. The hurricane would probably cause outages in both, not to mention the power.

The wind wasn't too bad yet, only the rain coming down harder in heavier and heavier sheets. She didn't hear from Houseboat or Mike throughout the day. No news is good news.

She ate an early dinner and prepared.

Six came faster than she expected, the time she both dreaded and anticipated. She wore jeans, a t-shirt, and her windbreaker over top, walking out into the rain. Her boots splashed through a couple inches of water here and there, the water piling up. The sky was dark, the sun slowly setting obscured by murky clouds. Soon it would be night.

She drove over to the police station, expecting some kind of trouble, knowing she was paranoid but refusing to dispel it. No one was out, though. Everyone on the island was hunkering down in face of the massive approaching storm.

Like normal people would do.

But they aren't normal. They have been replaced.

Moira found it hard to ignore the voice in her head that said, despite all the evidence, Blackwell Key was a normal place, filled with regular people. They weren't evacuating because of pure stubbornness, not because of obedience to their master.

But she knew it wasn't true. And in the few minutes as she headed to the police station, she felt the eyes on her from windows. She saw the old timers sitting on their porches, drinking and smoking, watching the rain intensify. The storm was entertainment now. A TV channel, airing their own destruction, and they were glued to the screen.

The parking lot was empty aside from the typical couple of cruisers and Mike's SUV. She parked next to him and headed inside, ducking from the rain. Felt like it had intensified in the five-minute drive over to the station.

Mike sat at the front desk, looking up at her entrance. His eyes were wide, and he looked concerned.

"You're early," he said.

"I don't think it makes a difference," she said. "Any problems?"

"No," said Mike. "Handoff for my shift was painless as always. Mark seemed normal. Said he was going to hunker down at his house overnight."

"I doubt that," said Moira.

"I doubt it too," said Mike. "But I didn't argue with him. He left right away."

"Where's Joan?" asked Moira.

"Still in her cell," he said. He reached below the desk and handed her a pistol. "Do you know how to shoot?"

"Yes," said Moira, taking it. "I've been to the range a few times."

"Have you ever shot at *someone*, though?" asked Mike.

"No," said Moira. "But knowing that the things I'll have to shoot at aren't human make it substantially easier."

"Fair enough," he said. "I've got another pistol and a riot gun stashed away, for Joan and Houseboat, plus ammo for everything."

"I hope we don't have to use it," said Moira.

"Me too," he said. "Let's go get Joan." He locked the front door, and then led her back into the cell areas, where Joan sat in the same place Moira had last seen her, days ago. Her eyes stared out into the middle distance until she realized Moira was there.

"Moira?" she asked. "Why are you here?"

"You didn't tell her?" asked Moira.

"No," said Mike. "She didn't need to know."

Moira looked to Joan. "We're breaking you out. We found evidence about Butch, about the creature you saw Bill become. Butch is behind it all. He's planning something big, and we need to stop him. You in?"

"Well, considering it gets me out of this cell, and keeps

me from drowning in the middle of the night, I'd say yes," said Joan, standing up. "Let's get the hell out of here."

Mike opened her cell, and Joan stepped out.

"So Butch is responsible?" she asked, following them back into the front of the station.

"Yes," said Moira. "We think he's converted most of the town into those things, like the one you killed."

"Fuck," said Joan. Something clicked in her eyes. Moira spotted it, a small change. She recognized it. Anger.

"It's worse," said Moira. "He's trying to awaken something else. Something bigger, during the hurricane."

"Well, fuck that," said Joan.

"Let me grab a few things and we can get out of here," said Mike. "We can meet up with Houseboat and head to Dagger Key." Mike ducked into a side office and came back out. He handed a shotgun to Joan. She weighed it in her hands and then racked it once.

"Oh, Mike," said a booming voice, walking into the central area. Butch stood there, a shotgun in his hands. His two other deputies flanked him, also carrying shotguns. "Arming a murderer with a police weapon. Tsk tsk tsk. Thought I could trust you."

Lightning crashed outside, and the building shook with thunder.

"Storm's here," said Butch, his smile wide, but this time, it was real, and the sight of it made Moira's hair stand on end. He would unhinge his jaw and swallow them whole. "Now you can all turn over your weapons, and head back to those cells, or you can get gunned down, right here, right now. Up to you."

"Fuck yourself," said Moira. Her pistol was tucked into

the back of her waistband. All they had to do was kill Butch, and this was over. But she wasn't fast enough. Only Joan had her weapon ready, and Moira didn't know if she understood what to do.

"I don't have all night," he said. "I got places to be."

No one said anything, and then one deputy shifted, and Joan swiveled and fired her shotgun in his direction, catching him in the shoulder, most of the shot hitting the corner of a cubicle wall.

"Down!" yelled Mike, and Moira dove to the floor, ducking behind a wall herself. Gunfire filled the space as everyone opened fire. Moira pulled her pistol from her waistband and glanced over. Joan had ducked behind a support pillar, the shotgun up tight against her. Joan nodded at her, and then counted down with her fingers. 3, 2, 1. And then she rolled out of the cover on the opposite side, firing immediately. Moira popped out of cover and saw the other deputy go down under Joan's fire. Mike fired his own pistol at the other deputy, who still stood, his shoulder bleeding.

Butch stood between them, his shotgun aimed at Joan. Moira aimed and fired, but only just as he fired. Joan yelled out in pain as his shot hit her. Moira didn't look, aiming at him. The gun barked in her hand, more recoil than she thought, but she corrected and fired three more rounds. One caught Butch in the chest, and he went down.

Mike's shots caught the other deputy in the heart, and he fell. Moira looked over, but couldn't see Joan.

"Joan?" she yelled.

"I'll survive," she yelled back.

Mike was already creeping up on the three men, his

gun ready to fire again. Moira followed his lead, moving past the small cluster of cubicles, waiting to see if the three men were still alive. The two deputies laid there, still, but Butch was gone. Mike was already moving out into the front area, but quickly returned.

"He's gone," said Mike.

"I hit him in the chest," said Moira.

"Not sure if that's enough to stop him," said Mike. He stared at the bodies of the two deputies. "I—I worked with these guys for years."

Joan limped up to them, leaning against the wall. Her hand was bloody.

"Joan," said Moira, walking toward her.

"I'm fine," she said. "It looks worse than it is. Some of the shot caught me in the ass. Hurts like hell but it won't kill me."

"That's something, at least," said Mike. "Let's go. Butch is surely heading for Dagger Key, and the storm is getting worse. Can you walk on your own, Joan?"

"I'll be fine," she said. They went to leave when they heard a noise behind them. They turned, almost in unison.

The two deputies shook on the floor like beached fish, their bodies popping up and down, their spines contorting.

"What the fuck?" asked Mike.

Their skin moved and shifted, softening, glistening now, the familiar sallow gray that Moira recognized. Their skin changed, their bones changed shape as they reformed inside. Mike watched as their faces melted away, revealing broad, featureless pates, large eyes and lipless mouths, gasping at the air.

"Now you see," said Moira. "Now you can see what they really are."

Their hands and feet were replaced by webbed claws, dripping with the viscous, deep sludge that Moira had drowned in her vision. The Servants forced themselves to their feet, their uniforms draped and baggy, half-fitting their malformed bodies. They turned toward the trio and rushed at them.

All three of them opened fire, raising their weapons and unleashing on the two of them. Joan fired three times with the riot gun, twice into one at near point blank range, and then one blast into the other. Moira and Mike fired the rest of their rounds into the other, popping it in the head and chest, each round impacting with a meaty thud. They both continued on unsteady legs, but then fell, leaking that same black liquid onto the floor of the police station, unmoving.

Joan stepped to one, racked a shell, and blew its brains out. She did it again with its brother.

"Can't be too sure," she said.

The storm raged outside. They left the gore of the police station behind them, with Joan leaning on Mike as they walked into the parking lot, the rain coming down in torrents. Blood soaked through her jail uniform, but was then soaked through with rain. Each of their steps splashed up water. Butch was already out of sight.

The wind whipped by them, and the palm trees danced in the air. It was getting worse quickly. They leaned against the wind.

"Let's use my SUV," said Mike. They all jumped inside,

out of the rain.

"What's the plan?" asked Joan.

"We need to get to Dagger Key," said Moira. "That's where Butch is heading."

"We need a boat then," said Joan.

"Houseboat is waiting for us," said Mike. "He'll get us to the island."

"What are we waiting for?" asked Joan. "Let's go."

Mike started the SUV and headed out of the parking lot. The vehicle shuddered as gusts of wind hit it, and Mike powered it through deep puddles, water splashing up and to the side.

"Jesus Christ," said Mike. "The low side of Blackwell is half-flooded already."

"Can we still get to Houseboat?" asked Moira.

"We should be able to," he said. "Anything online about where the storm is?"

"Towers are out," said Moira. "No service. No nothing."

"Well, that tells us something," said Mike. He turned onto US 1, the road deserted except for them and inches of water. The drainage ditches were already full to overflowing. "We don't have much time. The storm surge will hit soon. We need to be on a boat by the time that happens."

Mike piloted the vehicle through the rising waters, pulling off US 1 and down the street that led to the southern coast, where Seagull's sat. The SUV plowed through the water, hundreds of gallons splashing away with every foot traveled.

"Fuck," said Mike. "This is not good."

"We just have to get to Houseboat," said Moira. "We're

almost there."

Mike struggled to keep the SUV straight against the onrushing water, moving it past the few houses on the southern side of the island.

They saw Seagull's now, boarded up and abandoned. The cartoon seagull that graced the front sign shook and shimmied against the wind. The gravel parking lot was covered in six inches of water, the rain filling it higher with every second.

"Let's go, let's go," said Mike, and he jumped out of the vehicle, Joan and Moira following him, all carrying their weapons. Joan leaned against Mike again, still struggling from the shotgun blast, as they wound their way down around the side of the building, down the long wooden dock. Soon, they would see Houseboat, and they could get the hell out of here. Hopefully, he'd finished making his bomb, and they could blow the hell out of Dagger Key and Butch's plan.

The water was much higher below them than normal, all of them soaked to the bone in the rain. The wind howled through them, and Moira scrambled to her knees, trying not to get blown into the water.

"You alright?" asked Mike.

"I'll make it," she said, pushing herself to her feet.

They pushed down the dock, and then she paused.

"Fuck me," she said.

"Where is he?" asked Mike.

"I don't know," said Moira. The space where Houseboat had always docked was empty.

They had no boat, and no Houseboat.

23

"We need a boat!" yelled Joan. The rain was loud, especially here on the dock, hitting the surrounding water.

"The marina," said Mike. "My boat is there."

"Wait, where's Houseboat?" asked Moira.

"I don't know," said Mike. "But we can't wait here. Who knows what happened to him?"

"You don't think—"

"Think what?" asked Mike.

"That he's one of them," said Moira. "That he tricked us. That he tipped off Butch."

"I don't know," said Mike. "We have to move. Look." Mike pointed out over the water. The cloud cover and setting sun still provided enough light for Moira to see the incoming rain and clouds, darker even than what hovered over them.

"It's minutes now, not hours," said Mike. "Let's get back to the car."

They turned to head back and ran directly into someone. It wasn't a Servant, and it wasn't Houseboat.

It was Zeb.

"What are you doing here?" asked Moira.

"Houseboat told me to meet him here," said Zeb. He was soaked to the bone, wearing the same thing he wore when they met him before, but now also a weathered denim jacket. He stared at Moira.

"Who the hell is this?" asked Mike.

"This is Zeb," said Moira. "He got us the book."

"Houseboat told me you guys were trying to stop Butch, and to meet him here," said Zeb.

"Well, Houseboat is gone," said Moira. "And we're leaving."

They walked back down the dock, to the parking lot. The water level raised by the minute. The rainwater was ankle deep now, and both the rushing water and the wind pushed and pulled at them.

Zeb followed. "You can't just leave me," said Zeb. "I want to help."

"Get off the island," said Mike.

"You promised me, Moira," said Zeb, his voice as hard as she'd heard it so far. "You said I could help. I can help. Let me come with you."

"It's not safe, Zeb," said Moira, turning to look at him. "This isn't a game." He stared at her.

"I know," said Zeb. "I'm not joking."

Moira looked at Mike and Joan, both returning question mark looks. She looked back to Zeb. She remembered Houseboat's warning, but dismissed it. They couldn't just leave him. They needed the extra hands.

"Okay," she said. "You can come with us. But you do what we tell you."

"I will!" he said, jogging to join them through the rain and storm. They were all struggling to stay on foot with the wind.

Joan's face was a mask of pain and frustration, but she pushed through. She couldn't rely on Mike here, or they wouldn't be able to move at all. Moira herself struggled. She was the lightest one of them, and the wind was pushing her around. She struggled to not fall on her face into the water.

They got back to the car, the headlights still highlighting the pouring rain.

"Fucking goddamnit hell," said Mike, climbing behind the steering wheel. "It can never be easy. It can never be fucking easy." Joan and Moira climbed into the backseat, and Zeb jumped into the passenger seat. Mike didn't wait, slipping the car into drive and pushing forward. It lurched precariously at first, and then started moving, pushing hard through the climbing water.

"Thank God," said Joan.

"We get to the marina, and we use my boat," said Mike. "We should have done that in the first place."

"Houseboat has the bomb," said Moira. "We need it to destroy the obelisk."

"Well," said Mike. "Ain't shit we can do about that now. Guess we just have to kill Butch."

"I hit him in the chest, and it did nothing," said Moira.

"Doesn't mean he's invincible. If he was, he would have stood and fought," said Mike. "We can stop him. We can still stop him."

"Why would Houseboat abandon us?" asked Moira.

"Best not to think about it," said Joan. "He's always been a strange one. Just hope it was for a good reason, and not because he's one of those things."

Zeb's eyes danced between the three of them, but said nothing.

Mike struggled with the wheel as he pushed back up the street they had just driven down. The south side of the island was barely above sea level, and the barrage of rain had quickly flooded it. And that was without storm surge. The wind howled and Moira glanced out the window to see the cartoon seagull that adorned Seagull's fly past them, the weathered orange beak disappearing into the distance.

"Jesus," said Moira. Then she saw more movement. But it wasn't debris this time. It was a person, waving at them with raised arms, from a nearby roof. "Mike, stop."

"Why?" he asked. "If I stop, the water might take the SUV."

"It's Sarah," said Moira, pointing out the window. Sarah stood on a roof, waving her arms back and forth over her head, clearly yelling at the top of her lungs. "She needs help."

"She's one of those things," said Joan.

"I mean—it's hard to argue that she's not," said Mike. "After everything—"

Moira looked over at her, screaming for help from her roof. She was drenched, wearing similar clothes to what she wore at the community potluck. Was she one of the Servants? Or was she just some poor lady caught in the middle of this? Moira's stomach clenched. She couldn't live with herself, abandoning her, even with everything going on.

"How long until the hurricane makes landfall?"

"An hour," said Mike, looking at his watch.

"Stop," said Moira.

"One of those things?" asked Zeb. "Why are we stopping, then?"

"Moira, we don't have time—"

"We cannot let ourselves fall into apathy. We have to be human. It's all we have. We need to help her." She stared into Mike's eyes, and he stared back, and then wavered.

"Fine," he said. "But it's on you." He steered the SUV toward Sarah's house, driving up over the curb and onto the front lawn, where there was a little more water, jamming the SUV right up against the house with a thud.

"Let's get her," said Mike, and jumped out, the rain pouring down now, the wind forcing the car door open as soon as Mike cracked it. The interior of the SUV was immediately soaked, the water lapping up into the interior. Moira followed, and Joan did too, even as blood still leaked from her wound. Zeb climbed after them, looking up. Mike clambered up onto the hood of the car, and then reached up and hoisted himself up onto the roof. He pulled on the edge of the gutter, and it bent, held for a moment, and then pulled off in his hands, a stretch of the metal pulling off the roof.

"Oh, be careful, dear," said Sarah, sliding herself down to the edge of the roof.

"God-fucking-damnit!" yelled Mike, throwing the gutter aside. He picked himself up, standing back on the hood of the car.

"Can you jump down?" asked Moira.

"My hip—I can't," said Sarah. "I need help."

"Give me a second," said Mike. "I'll lower her."

The wind howled again, and Moira lost her footing, falling onto the hood herself, nearly sliding off. Joan grabbed her under her armpit, holding her there, even as she winced in pain.

"Kneel," said Joan. "Kneel until you need to stand."

"Are you okay?" asked Moira. "You're still bleeding."

"Oh, it hurts like hell," said Joan. "But I'll make it. As long as Butch is still standing, I'll make it." Moira stared at her for a moment, and saw the rage in Joan's eyes, simmering.

Mike hoisted himself up, and both Moira and Joan helped. Mike made it onto the roof, the storm howling around them. Zeb stood on the ground, holding both Moira and Joan stable.

"You shouldn't have come outside, Sarah," said Mike. "You should have evacuated."

"I thought it'd pass us by," she said. "It always passes us by."

Mike didn't answer that, only put his arms around her. "Get down on your butt, at the edge of the roof. I'll help guide you to Moira and Joan, okay?"

"Okay," said Sarah. She looked exhausted, her normally cheerful face full of pain and stress. She was soaked to the bone, standing out on her roof for so long.

"Oh, fuck," said Mike. Moira looked to him. He was

staring to the south.

"What is it?" asked Moira.

"Storm surge is coming! Hurry, hurry, hurry!" he yelled. Sarah slid down to the side of the roof, with her legs dangling over the edge. Moira and Joan stood to each side of her, and Mike stood behind her, his arms under her armpits. Sarah didn't weigh much, but still Mike strained as she slid off. Joan and Moira absorbed most of her weight, but still they fell into a heap on the hood of the SUV. Zeb kept them from falling into the water. Moira slipped again, and this time she fell into the rising water with a splash. She grunted with pain, and forced herself up. Mike hopped off the roof, onto the hood, onto the small area not occupied by Joan and Sarah. He slid, but stopped himself from going down, and then jumped down into the water with a massive splash. He went to Sarah, helping her down onto the ground, into the water, pushing her to the door.

"Let's go, let's go!" he yelled. They all jumped inside, everyone using all their might to close the doors against the howling wind. He slammed the car into reverse, out of Sarah's yard and back into the street, the car bumping as it crossed over the curb again. The car shimmied and slid as the current of water hit it again, rushing down the road.

"No no no no no," he said, slowly turning the wheel, pumping the gas strategically. He slammed it into four-wheel drive, and the tires found purchase and then the SUV crawled against the rising flood, thick torrents shooting out from underneath. Moira looked out the back window and she could *see* the storm surge, a tremendous rush of water slamming toward them.

"Go go go!" she said.

"I'm trying, I'm trying," he said. He pushed the gas harder, and the SUV pressed against the water. They drove forward, north, back toward the highway. "We can't stop. If we stop, the storm surge will take the car."

Moira looked back again, and she saw the water rushing toward them. They had predicted twenty feet of storm surge, and it was coming, enveloping the entire south side of Blackwell Key.

Mike pushed it as hard as he could, the SUV sliding back and forth as the currents of the water slid underneath the weight of the car. Debris flew by outside as the wind sped up behind them, ripping off shingles, siding, and entire roofs, flying past them. The wind caught the SUV, and it felt like a hand pushed them a few feet to the side.

"Oh fuck," said Joan.

"We're good, we're good," said Mike, as he steered into the wind. They approached the highway as the storm surge threatened to take them from behind. The SUV pushed up the incline up to the highway, and Mike gunned the engine even harder, and they drove up onto the highway and over to the other side. The storm surge slowed slightly as it met the incline, and then crossed over the highway. Moira looked back to see the southern side of Blackwell Key completely covered.

Sarah sat between Joan and Moira in the back seat, wringing her hands.

"I thought it'd pass us by."

24

They drove, the storm surge still pushing from behind them, the hurricane still encroaching. They had a few minutes.

"Where are we headed?" asked Sarah.

"The marina," said Mike. "We need a boat."

"That makes sense," said Sarah.

The wind howled around them, debris flying by intermittently. Mike pushed the vehicle through the heavy water, down one street, and then another, heading for the marina. A normally quick trip was taking three or four times as long, as the water pushed obstacles in the way, and slowed the vehicle. Still, they didn't have much time before the car wouldn't drive at all. They had to get to the marina first.

Moira caught some movement in her peripheral vision, something bobbing up and down in the water. She looked to catch it, but it was gone. It was probably nothing, probably a piece of debris trapped in the current.

But they hadn't seen any other people since they left the police station, aside from Sarah. Were they all sitting patiently in their living rooms, as their houses slowly filled with water? Wouldn't they be on their roofs at this point? The water was knee deep, even here on the north side, and it would fill up homes by the second.

The rain had only worsened, and it came down in torrents, heavy raindrops like bullets thudding down into the water.

"Oh Jesus Christ," said Mike, as he swerved suddenly. A car floated by them, a white sedan. It was a lighter car, sure, but it wouldn't be long before that was them.

"How far out are we?" asked Moira.

"A couple minutes," said Mike. "But I keep losing control." A gust of wind hit them and the SUV skidded to the side for a moment, and Mike swerved back before they hit a concrete mailbox. "Left at the next street, and then the marina will be at the end of the road."

The SUV pushed through the heavy water and Mike yanked the steering wheel to the left, and the headlights showed a long street of dark water. Lightning crashed and Moira saw the masts of the sailboats anchored in the marina, shaking in the night, and then the lightning disappeared. The dark had set in, heavy clouds covering any remaining sunlight.

Another car passed them on the left, going the other way, the water carrying it away, and Mike swerved again to miss it, forcing the wheel back the other way, desperately trying to maintain control of the big SUV. Its size was the only thing keeping it from floating away, and he gassed it hard. They were almost there. The wind howled around them, pushing harder and harder as the hurricane got closer and closer.

There was a great CRACK and Moira looked to see the roof pull off a home on the street, the wooden supports cracking under the immense pressure, and as soon as the wind was underneath it the rest broke as well, a series of gunshots, and the roof was gone, flying away in the wind. God forbid if it hit anyone, if it hit them. They'd be dead in an instant, a thousand pounds of wood flying at hundreds of miles per hour.

"No no no no no!" yelled Mike. Moira looked ahead, and huge tree leaned down across the road, too heavy to be moved by the water.

"We have to turn around," said Joan.

"We can't," said Mike. "There's no way the SUV will make it. Fuck!" He pounded the steering wheel once. The headlights shone on the tree and there was no way around it. "We have to go the rest of the way on foot."

"On foot?" asked Moira. "You mean swim."

"We have to swim?" asked Zeb.

"Whatever it is," said Mike. "We have to get there. It's the only way we have left. It's not too far. We can do it."

"Can you handle that, Sarah?" asked Moira.

"Maybe if I have some help," she said, her face full of fear.

"You stick with me, Sarah," said Mike. "We'll go together. Grab your guns and try and keep them dry." Joan slung her shotgun around her neck, and then grabbed the bag full of ammo, and did the same with it. "Everyone ready? Let's go."

They pushed the doors open and stepped down into the water, now above their knees. The storm surge was somewhere behind them, pushing its way through the island, and they didn't have much time before it overwhelmed them. Still, the marina was only a few hundred yards away. Easy peasy, if it wasn't raining—

If it wasn't raining, you'd just drive there.

Moira stepped through the water. Joan followed her, grimacing through her pain, but keeping up. Mike and Sarah pushed through it as well, Mike's arm around her. Zeb followed them all, trudging his skinny frame through the heavy water. The rain pelted them, and the wind pushed and pulled against them. It blew hard, but Moira leaned against it, and made headway against the wind. They reached the tree, mounting the thick trunk and climbing over, out of the water and back in.

Moira only heard the rain, and the wind, and the sound of her own breathing. She was soaked to the bone, her clothes sticking to her, and her shoes squelched with every step. She looked back, and Joan was right behind her, holding the bags with ammo and flashlights. Joan had taken one out and flashed it in front of them, enough to see, illuminating the water as it bubbled and toiled. Mike was still helping Sarah down from the tree, grabbing her and putting her back down into the water, the wind cutting at all of them. A piece of siding flew past her, and her heart jumped at the near call.

There was no dodging the debris, only hoping it

wouldn't catch you. It was a deadly game they were playing. One stray piece of wood, of shingle, of metal, and they would be killed instantly.

"Keep pushing!" yelled Mike. "We're almost there!"

An unfamiliar noise entered Moira's hearing.

"What is that?" she asked.

"The storm surge!" yelled Joan. "Move!"

Moira pushed hard, leaning against the wind, trudging through the high water. Her thighs burned as she pushed, and she couldn't imagine the pain that Joan was dealing with. Moira didn't look back, moving as fast as she could. She saw the outlines of the masts against the night sky, slim, dark shadows, and they could get there. Another minute, and they'd be there.

And then the storm surge hit, and she was knocked off her feet. She fell, and then was underwater, as the water hit her in the back, hard, and she tried to find her way back to the surface. Up was down and down was up, and her feet found the ground, and then a hand grabbed her wrist and pulled her back up. Joan was there, and had saved her. The storm surge was still coming, the water up to their necks.

"Where's Mike and Sarah?" asked Moira. They both looked back, and Sarah was perched on the tree, the water desperately pushing at it, the tenuous connection to its trunk the only thing keeping it from flowing away. Mike stood next to her, staring at them.

"We have to keep going!" he said. "Or we'll die here." He looked exhausted. The water continued to rise, and within a minute, they'd be swimming. The current already threatened to push her away, her hold on to Joan the only thing keeping her standing.

Then something brushed against her leg.

"Did you feel that?" asked Moira.

"Feel what?" asked Joan.

"I don't know," said Moira, yelling over the wind and rain. "Something—"

And then she felt something grasp for her ankle, and she screamed. "They're in the water!" She pulled her leg away and moved back to the tree.

"What—"

"The Servants! They're in the water! We have to get out of the water!"

Mike stared at her, looking past her to the marina, for only a split second, and then scanned their surroundings. "The house. We can get on the roof. It's all we have."

Moira nodded and swam toward the nearby house. The tree had been planted in its front yard, and its roof was only twenty or so feet away. They all swam as hard as they could. Moira got there first. She bobbed up and down in the water and then pushed herself up and out, able to grab onto the edge of the arch that extended over their front door. She dragged herself up, hoping it would hold her weight, and it did, and she got her feet up and out of the water, away from the hands grasping at her underneath it. Moira climbed up onto the roof and then looked back to see Joan following her. Mike swam after them, helping Sarah as much as he could. Zeb was behind them all, struggling in the water. He wasn't prepared for this. Sarah was fighting with all her might against the tide. Mike stayed within distance of her and pulled her to the wall of the house as he got closer. Moira and Joan extended a hand and pulled her up onto the roof, and Mike followed.

Zeb came last, and they pulled him up like a drowning rat. They all huddled close to the shingled roof, sheltering as much as they could from the harsh wind.

Moira hoped the wind wouldn't take the roof.

"Fucking hell," said Joan. "All the guns are soaked. Who knows if they'll fire."

"From one roof to another," said Sarah, her eyes stunned.

"What do we do?" asked Moira, staring at Mike.

"One of us should swim for it," said Mike. "Get to a boat, and bring it back for the others. Then we can head to Dagger Key. It has to be me. I can get to my boat and bring it back."

"You'll never make it," said Moira. "It's a suicide mission." Moira grabbed a flashlight from Joan's bag and shone it over the rising water. It rushed by them, even higher than it was, the storm surge taking over the island. It was all underwater now, over their heads. And god knows what lie underneath.

"Butch can't succeed," said Mike. "We have to try. I'm the only one not injured, and knows where my boat is. I can do it. I'll get there and be back in a few minutes."

"They're in the water, Mike!" yelled Moira, over the howling wind. It had picked up again. The eye was close, and the strongest winds were pelting them now. Moira ducked her head against the gale as debris flew around them. "You won't make it a hundred feet!"

"I have to try!" he yelled back. "Keep the weapons, stay here. If I don't come back—I'm sorry for not believing you." Mike held her eyes for a long second, and then went to the edge of the roof, getting ready to dive in, staring at the water. He prepared to jump.

"Wait!" yelled Moira. "Don't."

"Moira—"

"Mike. Look," she yelled, over the din. She moved her light to what she had seen.

Her light focused on a shape as it bobbed in the water. Sallow, gray flesh, soft, tinged with toxic darkness. A wide, open mouth, filled with tiny teeth. Featureless soft eyes. First one, and then a second, and a third, and then a fourth, and then too many to count.

"They've been following us," said Moira. "They've known all along."

"Back up," said Mike. They all moved back to the middle of the roof, up along the peak. The creatures mounted the building, pulling themselves up. Moira swallowed, pulling her pistol from the back of her pants.

"Here they come."

25

The Servants emerged from the water and climbed onto the roof, slimy webbed hands gripping the gutters, the shingles, the eaves, and pulling themselves up, one after the other.

The humans on the roof each shone a flashlight at the creatures as they piled onto the house, their black viscous sweat protecting them from the rain. Their eyes stared at them, dull and expressionless, their skin heaving with troubled breath. They had two arms, two legs, but the gray skin had pulled back against the bones, the flesh hanging in places, left over from the transformation back and forth. Moira saw their gills on their neck, the creatures used to breathing underwater.

Not underwater. Under the black tar of another plane.

They were all naked, formless, shedding their human clothes along with their forms. They had bid their time, waiting until the right moment to strike, buying valuable time for their master. Butch was heading to or at Dagger Key right now, waiting for the hurricane and soon it would be here, and he could complete his dark ritual. He had changed most of the island for this moment, getting ready for this day. The Servants would take the island for him and maintain control. They would quash any dissent, any rebellion, by the endless number of them crawling from the water.

The wind blew and howled, gusting hard and each time Moira ducked against the roof, avoiding being thrown off, back into the water. The creatures didn't sway, didn't move, the Servants immune to the effects. More and more of them pulled themselves out, standing there in the darkness, all staring at the five humans trapped in the middle of the roof.

"What are they?" asked Sarah.

"They're your neighbors," answered Moira, and then they charged, rushing them en masse.

"Stay behind us, Sarah," said Mike, pulling out the riot gun and firing. They all fired, hoping the rounds would still work after being submerged and rained on. Moira fired as they approached, aiming for center mass, hoping it would be enough to stop them. Joan stood next to her, shooting with her riot gun, racking after each shot, the sound of gunfire joining the cacophony of the storm. The creatures fell, one after the other, as bullets and shells hit them. Some rolled down the roof and slid back into the water. Others only stumbled or dropped to their hands and knees.

"Give me a weapon!" yelled Zeb.

"There's nothing to give!" yelled Mike, back. Zeb hung back with Sarah.

More climbed out of the water, the entire population of Blackwell Key here, surrounding them. Moira emptied her clip, popped it out, and grabbed three more from the ammo bag. They were slick in her hand, and even if they hadn't fallen in the water, the heavy rain would endanger them firing. But they had nothing else.

Joan took a stack of shells from the bag and reloaded as Moira covered her, and then Joan did the same for Mike, the creatures coming in waves, the sunken, softening flesh exploding with each shot, black viscous blood pouring from their wounds, staining the roof. Moira smelled it, even through the wind and rain, the smell of sulfur and brimstone. It burnt her nostrils, even as the wind howled around her, the rain falling into her eyes, obscuring her vision.

The weather continued to get worse, the rain somehow falling even harder, the sky letting go of all the water in the world, dropping in sheets on top of them. The wind threatened to blow them away. Moira fell to her butt. Anything to not fall off. Sarah cowered between all of them, her hands over her ears, blocking out the terrible deafening gunshots. Moira's ears rang with each shot, but she couldn't stop, not now. If they would stop Butch, they would have to drive them back.

Debris flew past them, and Moira did her best to ignore it, knowing there was nothing she could to dodge or avoid it. Branches, mailboxes, lawn ornaments, and siding soared by, fiddling through the wind, becoming deadly missiles for anything standing in the way. A stop sign whizzed by her head and sliced through one of the creatures, the top third of its body falling away from the rest, black liquid pouring out of both sides.

Moira lost count of the creatures they killed, because they kept replacing themselves. Still, they fired, hoping against hope that they could somehow kill them all.

She pulled the trigger, over and over, but then the gun clicked dully, and she realized she had found the first dud. Moira cleared the round from the gun and fired again, but it clicked dully again, and then the creature hit her, sick and wet on top of her. She reached up and grabbed its wrists as it tried to wrap its webbed hands around her throat. Its black excretions dripped past her face, and she smelled its horrible odor now, so close to her, as they slid down the side of the roof.

Its wide, hideous mouth was right in front of her, ready to swallow her up, rows and rows of tiny teeth like a shark, ready to engulf her, ready to chew her into little pieces. The Servant made no sound, other than its labored breath, each exhalation a ball of vile air, full of death and poison. She coughed, and her eyes watered, and her arms trembled, trying to keep it away from her. It drew closer and closer, and soon it would eat her, swallow her whole, drag her under the water, and she would be in the purview of the Great Beast, and—

A shotgun blast rang out, and the creature's head evaporated as Joan shot at point blank range. Black matter spilled out onto her, and she closed her eyes and mouth, turning her head, hoping to keep it away from her. It only hit her clothes, luckily. She didn't want to know what would happen if she swallowed it. She opened her eyes and threw the body of the creature off of her, scrambling to her feet just in time to see Joan get tackled by one of the things. Joan slammed it in the head with the butt of the riot gun, once, twice, and Moira reloaded, slamming in a new clip, hoping the bullets in this weren't duds.

Joan smashed the creature with the stock of the shotgun a final time and threw it off her, and Moira fired once, twice into its head, the bullets working this time. Mike had paused to reload and Moira moved past Sarah and Zeb to cover him, as several more creatures charged. She fired smoothly, the rounds hitting the monsters in the neck and chest. They fell soundlessly, sliding down the roof and back into the water.

They had cleared the roof for now, and they hurriedly reloaded.

"Protect the roof," said Mike. "Don't let them climb up."

They spread out slightly, enough to get to the edges, and fired as any of the creatures showed their head, either killing or wounding them before they could mount onto the roof. After a few moments, they stopped trying to get up, doing their best to avoid the gunfire. The bodies of the voidborn bobbed in the rising water, dozens of them surrounding the house on all sides.

The wind howled around them, and they pivoted back and forth, all of them scanning along the roof line.

"See any more of them?" yelled Mike.

"No," said Joan.

"They've gone back underwater!" yelled Moira, as she continued to scan the edge of the water. The rain poured down on top of them, and she could barely hear the others. The wind blew hard and Moira braced herself against the roof. It was still picking up, and she didn't know how much longer they could stay up here. The roof rattled below her as the wind got under the eaves, and sooner rather than later it would be torn off, with them on top of it.

"We can't stay up here forever!" she yelled.

"We hold it for now!" yelled Mike. "It's all we—"

And then he yelled, a terrible, piercing noise. The sound of pain. Moira and Joan turned to look simultaneously.

A creature was biting Mike on his neck, its wide mouth gnawing at him.

Oh no.

It somehow had slipped between them and gotten behind them. But how?

And then Moira realized. Zeb was missing. It wore his clothes.

Because he was one of them.

26

Mike struggled against the Zeb creature, but it was latched onto his neck, gnawing with row after row of tiny teeth. They couldn't shoot it, they might hit Mike, and they ran over to him, the rain pouring on them. Lightning crashed as Joan slammed the butt of her shotgun into the back of its head, over and over again, until it finally let go, and then she jammed the gun up against its skull and fired, the thing that pretended to be Zeb falling over, dead. It slid down to the edge of the roof and into the water.

How? When?

They had gotten the book not three days ago from Zeb. A Servant wouldn't have given them that, no way no how. Zeb had been so excited to help. He had wanted to—

Wanted to infiltrate the marina.

He had gone and gotten caught, and Butch saw his chance. He replaced him then.

"Motherfucker," said Moira, going to Mike, who had slumped down, holding his neck. He half laid on the peak of the roof, blood trickling through his fingers. Moira crouched next to him. "Cover us. They'll come up again." Moira didn't look at Joan, but Joan was already firing the riot gun, racking it after every shot, the sound of the shotgun blasts intermixed with thunder. Sarah was there with them. She held a small cloth to Mike's neck.

She looked over at Mike. His eyes were sunken, his flesh pale. He held a hand to his neck. "Let me see," said Moira, tugging at Sarah's hand. Sarah pulled it away, and she saw the damage.

Oh hell.

The damage was catastrophic. The Servant's teeth had torn away a terrible amount of flesh from Mike's shoulder and neck, and blood poured from the wound. But it had missed the carotid. He might make it. She hurriedly ripped at his shirt, pulling away a long stretch of cloth.

"This will hurt," she said, and then wrapped it tightly around the damage, tying it off. Mike grimaced.

"Sarah, try and keep the bleeding down," said Moira. Sarah nodded, and tended to Mike's neck.

"Take my shotgun," he said, his voice weak. "I'll take the pistol. Can still fire that." Moira nodded and traded him quickly, rising back to her feet and seeing where they were.

Where they were was dire. Joan had been firing as she had been tending to Mike, but the creatures had continued their onslaught, reclaiming territory they had ceded earlier. Now the roof teemed with the things, even as Joan blasted them. Moira covered the other side, and shot as well, but they just kept coming, and as Mike peppered them with pistol shots, they fell. But they had still killed less than a hundred, and the entire population of Blackwell Key hid out in the water, pushing away the dead, bobbing in the rising, turbulent waters.

"We can't keep up with this," said Moira.

"I'll stop when I'm dead," said Joan, racking another shot. "Cover me while I reload." She grabbed another fistful of shells from the bag and slid them into the riot gun. "That's the last of it. Make them count."

Moira did the best she could. It was hard to miss them, even in the scattered light of their flashlights, with the wind and rain. There were just so many. Moira fired, pumped, fired again, over and over, all these shells working, no misfires, and she sent these terrible things back to the void where they came from. The abyss could have them back, their dark viscous blood spilling out. They slid down the roof and piled at the eaves, their thick blood mixing with the rainwater like an oil spill.

There was a scream, and they all looked to see Sarah being dragged away. They fired at the creatures surrounding her, but for every one they killed, two took its place.

"Motherfuckers!" yelled Joan, and then Sarah was gone, underwater. She was human, and they had taken her. Moira's stomach sank. Moira fired and fired, and then her gun was empty.

Joan and Mike had already run out of ammo, and they had watched her fire her last remaining shells. The creatures still pulled themselves out of the water. There were so many, hundreds and hundreds, and they surrounded the four of them. And they knew now the guns were empty, and they pulled onto the roof, stacked a dozen deep in every direction.

The wind howled hard, and both Joan and Moira crouched as not to be blown away, the wind hitting them, cutting from the speed, but the Servants of the Deep were unaffected. They stood staring with expressionless faces, with dark, dead eyes.

They knew that the trio was helpless now.

"Come on, you motherfuckers!" yelled Joan. She held the shotgun like a club, ready to swing at any that came close.

The creatures stared, their broad mouths opening wide, wider still.

"Fuck me," said Mike.

BANG

A shot rang out over the din of the rain and the wind. A soft thud followed and a Servant fell. Another shot followed, and another, loud cracks in the dark, and two more Servants fell. They turned and looked to the sound, as three more shots rang out in sequence.

BANG BANG BANG

Three more Servants dead, their heads jolting back, and then falling to the roof, sliding into the sea. Moira looked and saw the recognizable floodlights slowly pulling toward them.

Houseboat.

Shot after shot rang out, as the creatures fell, and then they turned and rushed toward the water to get out of the line of sight. His voice rang out over the water.

"Get ready!" Houseboat yelled, his boat in view now. "They'll be coming for the boat!"

Moira and Joan leaned down and got Mike to his feet. They walked to the edge of the roof, their feet at the edge of the gutter. The water still rose, and soon it would be over the rooftop. The bodies of the creatures bobbed up and down in the water, and Moira tried to not look at them. Who had they been, once upon a time? How long had they lived with a different skin?

Houseboat pulled up, the boat smashing into the gutters of the house.

"Hope they don't bill me for that," he said. "Hurry. They're probably gathering around us right now."

They helped Mike aboard, and Moira and Joan followed. As they pulled away, a creature wrapped its webbed fingers over the edge of the boat, followed by another and another.

"Goddamnit!" yelled Houseboat. "Here, help." He extended a crowbar to Joan, and she grabbed it, slamming into the creatures as they tried to board the boat. Moira looked around and saw a large pocketknife, and she snatched it, sinking it deep into a creature as it pulled itself aboard. Black blood spilled onto the deck, and Moira pulled it out, the creature falling back into the water.

Mike sat back against the cabin as they drove off the creatures, Moira and Joan hacking and beating anything that tried to board. Houseboat got behind the wheel and steered away.

The last creature fell into the water, and they pulled away from the roof of the house.

27

Houseboat drove them away from the rooftop, and the rain crashed down. Moira saw the boats bobbing in the marina, straining at their moorings as the water rose above the docks.

The boat shuddered as the wind gusted, and Houseboat steered into it, the boat turning and shaking. A little bit harder and it would have capsized them.

"Fucking hell," said Houseboat, his eyes ahead of them. The floodlights cast a halo around them as they left Blackwell Key behind.

"Where were you?" asked Moira. "You were supposed to pick us up!"

"Those bastards ambushed me," said Houseboat. "They were people from town, at first. They told me to leave, get out before the storm got bad. When I told them no, they changed—changed into those things. Right in front of me. And I believed you, Moira, I really did, but seeing them, right in front of your face, well—"

"It's a different thing entirely," said Moira. "I know."

"So I got the hell out of there," said Houseboat. "Figured I would circle back around, but they were waiting for me, basically at every dock. Was thinking I'd go to Dagger Key on my own, and do what I could, but then I heard the gunshots. Is Mike okay?"

"I don't know," said Moira. She looked out. The storm howled around them. The halo of lights illuminated the pouring rain, lightning cracking through the sky, followed by thunder. With every gust of wind, the boat would shake and shudder. "Can the boat handle this?"

"As long as I steer into it," said Houseboat. "Wind's over 100 now, regularly. It's gusting to 150." His eyes didn't leave the water ahead and the front of the boat. "I'm doing my best."

Joan came in, Mike leaning heavily on her. She set him down in a chair, where he collapsed.

Moira studied him under the lights of the boat. His eyes were sunken, the layers of shirt that covered his wound soaked through with blood. He had aged 30 years in a few hours. His skin was gray and pale, and his hands shook softly in his lap. Even worse, black streaks were popping up all over him. Moira quickly realized those were his veins. Whatever the bite of that thing did, it was killing him.

"How are you feeling?" asked Moira.

"Like shit," said Mike. "Jesus Christ. What a nightmare.

I was going to see my aunt and uncle up in Ft. Myers this weekend. Hang out, do some retired people stuff. It was going to be fun." He stared at Moira. "Don't think that'll be happening now, huh?"

"I don't know," said Moira. "Maybe we'll blow this thing up, stop Butch, and everything will be hunky dory."

He raised his hand in front of his face. "That thing did something to me, Moira. I don't think the bite alone would have done anything, you know? It hurt like hell, and I lost some blood, but it wasn't too deep, and it missed the artery. But it carries something. I don't know, but it's inside me. I can feel it."

"Just hold on," said Moira.

"I'm doing my best," said Mike. "Houseboat. Is that the bomb?" Mike had cast his gaze to a small package on the table, right where Houseboat had made his model ship, in what seemed like a lifetime ago. But it had only been a few days.

"It sure as hell is," said Houseboat. "Enough explosive to take out the whole fucking island."

"That might be overkill," said Moira.

"You said that monolith might be made of iron. So I planned for the highest stress tolerances I could find. It was a fun build," said Houseboat. The boat shuddered again, and hit a wave, the houseboat flying into the air, and wind was underneath them for a terrifying second, and then they collided with the water with a terrible thud. They all braced themselves.

"We'll make it," said Houseboat. "Darling can take anything this storm throws at her. I told you. Although turning toward Dagger Key is going to be a problem."

"What do you mean?" asked Joan.

"As long as I'm steering into the wind, we're doing just fine," he said. "But as soon as I turn, so we can board the island, we'll be sailing perpendicular to it. And that won't be good. Might capsize us."

"What are our options?" asked Moira.

"Two option. Hope or pray," said Houseboat. "Which one you pick is up to you, depending on your particular belief in a god or gods."

"How long before we have to turn?" asked Moira.

"Not very long," said Houseboat. "The wind is slowing us down, but Dagger Key isn't that far away."

"What's the plan when we get there?" asked Joan.

"You and I try and stop Butch by whatever means necessary. Houseboat arms the bomb, and then we get the hell out of there."

"Can we stop him?" asked Moira. "I hit him—"

"We do what we can," said Joan. "At worst, we keep him busy. I don't think he can pull it off without that thing you described."

The wind picked them up, and they slammed down again, and all of them braced for impact. The boat made a massive cracking sound.

"Don't think Darling will be living a long and happy life after tonight," said Houseboat.

"She just has to hold a few minutes longer," said Moira. "How much longer?"

"I was about to say," said Houseboat. "We need to turn now. But be ready. Things could fall apart at any moment. I'll do my best. I'm going to turn us and then hit the throttle as hard as I can. We'll see what Darling can take. You all ready?"

They all shared a glance and gave Houseboat a nod. "Alright then. Hold on."

Houseboat spun the wheel suddenly, the halo of light turning, and threw the throttle as hard as he could. Moira heard the motor rev up, the propeller spinning up hard and fast beneath them. The boat shook as gusts of wind hit them from the side. Houseboat stayed behind the wheel, his eyes still focused on the window ahead of him.

Moira watched him as he steered slightly into the wind, trying to avoid getting capsized. Moira grabbed onto the side of the cabin. Everyone else did the same, even Mike, who looked worse by the moment.

"I think she's going to take it," said Houseboat, a smile on his face. "My little old lady is strong enough, after—"

A terrible gust flew past them and the boat shook, and then the roof of the cabin was gone, ripped off in one swoop, the force of wind getting underneath it and pulling it off. The wood cracked and snapped and it disappeared, and rain pelted them, their drying clothes soaked again in an instant. There was no more shelter, only a few lights remaining on the front of the boat.

"We can't stop!" yelled Houseboat, behind the wheel. Blood flowed down his face from a wound on his forehead, opened up when a stray piece of wood sliced him as it passed. The boat shook again as another gust ripped through them, the boat tumbling to one side. Houseboat corrected and steered into it at the last second, and they rolled back to normal position. The motor still roared, churning through the rising water as fast it could go. The cacophony of the storm filled Moira's ears, and she looked out into the darkness, seeing swirling rain and seas.

"How close are we?" she yelled, crouching, bracing herself against the small part of the boat that remained. Half of the cabin had vanished along with the roof, blown away in an instant by the wind. It assaulted them all, all of them holding as best they could. Houseboat still stood behind the wheel, wind and rain pelting him in the face. He stood his ground. Moira looked out and swore she saw Dagger Key, distant, but that was impossible. It was too dark.

"Close!" he said. "Another minute, and we'll be there! I'm going to ram right into the shore, just beach it. We'll have to brace for impact, but there's no way we can slow down and—"

And then another gust hit them as they rose on a wave, and the boat rolled, and Houseboat tried to correct, but he was too late.

Time slowed down. Moira looked at Joan, who dove to the bomb. Mike held onto the side of his chair, his fingertips lined with black, his face full of fear. Houseboat reached for a life preserver. The boat went vertical, and Moira felt gravity shift below her as the boat turned over, falling on top of all of them, and then she was beneath the waves.

28

Moira was thrown into the turmoiled water. She dove into the darkness, immediately realizing the boat would be behind her, and she needed to swim down and away from it. The impact hit above her, and she swam as hard as she could, into the darkness. She opened her eyes in the salt water, and it burned, the salt eating at her, but she saw nothing, the small lights of the houseboat disappearing as it sank.

She was alone in the water, swirling around her as she fought for breath. She pushed, kicking, and then she realized.

Moira wasn't in water anymore. No, she was in the other substance, dark and thick, the natural home of the Servants, the home of The Beast That Dwelled Beneath The

Waves. The space between their two worlds was thin here, near the coast, near the edge of the land, where you could walk down into the ocean and never return, and here, near here is where it slept, and she saw everything now.

She was drowning, and she saw everything.

She saw Butch. But he wasn't Butch then. He was Archibald, or Archie to his friends. At least when he had friends. He had left them all behind ever since he had gone diving. A daredevil lark introduced to him by his uncle, who had bought the rig with some winnings from a poker game. The diving suit was primitive, especially compared to today, but it worked, worked well enough. They tested it out, Archie and his uncle, out to a small pond, and they had gone out to the middle of the pond, and Archie had stepped out into the water, the heavy suit sinking straight down to the bottom, only ten feet deep.

When it's only ten feet, you don't think too much about it. If there's a rip in the suit, or a kink in the oxygen hose, then you just walk back onto shore and open up the faceplate. But it worked, and they didn't need to do anything. And it was incredible to Archie. He was still young then, fresh out of college, working for his father's bank, ready to take over the reins whenever his father retired. It would be awhile yet, but until that day, Archie would have a good job, easy, and that paid well.

But it was boring. Desperately boring. Girls, alcohol, they only went so far, especially after a while. And his father expected him to settle down. Archie had put it off, and he knew Father and Mother were waiting, and it was only a matter of time before Father put his foot down, and then Archie would find some sow to mate with. But then

Uncle Franklin came to him with this diving suit, and down there on the bottom, everything disappeared. Down there in the darkness, there was nothing but him and the deep. Even in the pond. But the pond wouldn't do, no, not for long.

They lived in New York, and soon they were chartering boats, and going to the ocean, and testing the limits of the suit. Deeper and deeper they would go. And Archie saw the worry on Uncle Franklin's face, worry that he'd send down his only nephew to the sea floor, and then something would rupture, and he'd have to tell his older brother that Archie didn't make it back, and he would have no heir for his name.

Archie didn't care. There was no worry for failure of the equipment. The reward of being down there was much too great, no worry about equipment failure, or of the bends. The deeper they went, the better. The ocean floor was the only place he could find peace, find solace for his scattershot mind. The desperate clawing for attention, for excitement, for contentment—it all went away while he was down there. It was the only time he could truly be alone.

His last trip with his uncle wasn't much different than any of the others. They were going a little deeper, and Uncle Franklin had been worried about it, but Archie had dismissed his fears as foolish. There was always a chance of an accident, he had told Franklin, and they had gone, anyway. When Archie had something in mind, there was no stopping him. There was no talking him out of it, especially for Franklin, who was never as skilled at negotiation as his banker brother.

And so they went, and everything was going normally. Archie had jumped over the edge of the charter ship. The sea was a little wild that day, but nothing crazy, and Archie had quickly forgotten his uncle's worries as soon as he hit the water and began to sink. The darkness enveloped him, and soon, he was on the bottom, hundreds of feet down, his lone light the only source of illumination, the only light that land had seen, ever. He looked around, and walked, slowly stepping in a direction. Some fish absentmindedly swam past him, but largely the bottom was empty, a barren desert of sand, with an occasional crab or lobster scurrying past.

And then he did something, something he did often, but of which he never told anyone.

He turned off his headlamp, leaving him in total darkness. His forced breathing, his hurried heart rate, it immediately slowed. He was no longer a stranger, down in the dark, down in the deep. Now he was a companion of the darkness. Now he *belonged*.

Just as he had told no one about exploring down there, he had never told anyone about what he discovered down there. Or to be more accurate, what he felt down there, with the light off.

Because he didn't feel alone. In fact, it was the only time in his life that he *didn't* feel alone. It was the only time he felt close to anything, felt a kinship with anyone. His parents, his family, his friends. They felt alien to him. They felt distant.

Down there, he felt *something*, something loving and accepting. It embraced him, the darkness, and the thing that lived in it.

And he felt that warmth, that embrace, and then water

replaced the oxygen, suddenly, the rush of air disappearing, replaced with liquid, and he was drowning. He looked up, to see what the problem was, but there was nothing but that darkness. And as his lungs filled with water, that's all there was. Nothing but darkness, and the thing down there in it.

Archie woke up on the deck of the chartered boat, his uncle staring at his face. They had pulled him up, and dragged him out of the clunky suit, and had pumped his chest until his heart started again. Archie coughed up the gallon of water in his lungs, and it hurt. They had broken some of his ribs. But he looked to his uncle, and the distant feeling he had always felt toward his family had amplified, had grown. Because he didn't see his uncle anymore. In fact, he felt only disgust toward him, and every other human.

Because The Beast had spoken to him then, while he stood dying in the deep, and shown him the way. And diving no longer interested Archie. Many thought it was the near death experience that had driven him away, but no, he had realized that diving would never get him as close to The Sleeper as he wanted. And so he searched, in forgotten libraries and rare books, among all the occultists and eccentrics. And he found reports of communication with something half asleep, something waiting at the bottom of the world.

And so he settled Blackwell Key, after a windfall, a *tragic accident* befalling his parents, and his uncle, he being the sole inheritor. He settled Blackwell Key, giving business ventures over to managers, taking the profits and building in the Keys, where the water was warmer. And he researched, and he found the way in.

Moira saw all of this as she struggled in the dark, deep, and she saw now it was her drowning that did, that allowed her the connection to this place, this other world, a plane made of viscous darkness, where the Servants lurked, where The Great Beast had once lived, and now they wanted a different home, and they would wait for it, and influence those it thought it could.

And those same tendrils reached out to her. They could save her. They could embrace her. She would be a master and commander of this new world. No more fighting for lost causes. No more being shunted aside. They would hang on her every word, every missive a directive. No more asking about belief. Her word would become belief.

It reached out and pulled at her. And the power tempted her. She wanted that strength, that authority. A part of her craved it, wanted vengeance for years of yelling at the top of her lungs at a disaffected audience that ignored her, that killed the world. Leaving her and her words in the dark.

It tempted her.

But no. No, she could never embrace that thing for what it was, for the bald power it represented. The power came with a cost, a human cost, both for her and the world.

She swam away, back to the surface, her lungs straining as she ran out of the oxygen, desperately kicking, urgently clawing against the dark water—

And then she was on the surface again, the water bobbing as the storm swirled overhead. The rain smashed into the surface of the ocean, and the waves threatened to push her back under, but she kicked. She looked for anyone, but it was too dark.

"Houseboat! Joan! Mike!" she yelled, but no one answered. She could barely hear her own voice over the din of the wind and rain. She needed to find land. It wasn't too late.

She looked, waiting for the wave to push her up, and looked, and she saw the light, the dim light cast by Dagger Key. She saw it for a moment, but she didn't wait, swimming hard in that direction, summoning all of her strength. Being in the water sapped her, but she reached deep for the last of her reserves. If she didn't get out of the water, she would die here, and Butch would succeed with his ritual, and he would awaken the Beast, the Beast that would change the world.

She swam, kicking and paddling, trusting her gut, heading to the light. Her heart beat hard in her chest, her lungs gasping, but she swam away from the dark water, away from the pain, away from the welcome embrace of the Sleeper.

Moira swam, and then her feet hit something, and she realized it was the cypress trees. They were underwater now, the storm surge taking most of Dagger Key away. She moved past them, the upper boughs over the top of the water here, as the island sloped up. She found the ground below her, and she walked, the trees shaking back and forth around her, grabbing onto the trunks as the wind hit her.

And then she was at the edge of the trees, and she saw the obelisk, and she saw Butch.

29

Butch stood in front of the obelisk, the storm swirling around him, the rain and wind battering him. He stood unaffected, his arms above his head, reaching to the sky, hailing to the monolith, hailing That Which Dwells Beneath The Waves. He wore a black robe, soaked through with rain.

He was alone now, his deputies killed, his Servants left behind. Only he worshiped. His voice rang out over the chaos and cacophony of the storm as he screamed and wailed in an alien language, his teeth gnashing, spitting saliva with every gnarled breath that leapt from his throat.

She crawled out of the water, the torches surrounding Butch the only light, burning despite the wind and the rain. Her lungs ached from her terrible swim. But there was no one else.

She had no weapons. What could she do?

No, she had one weapon in her zipper pocket. She reached down and pulled it out, the pocketknife. A four-inch blade. It wasn't much, but it would be enough. She unfurled the knife and circled around Butch. He didn't see her, he only saw the monolith now, only saw The Beast. Its arrival was imminent. She crept behind him, all her movements hidden by the storm. The wind rushed by her, but here, it didn't push her. The wind was over 150 now, with gusts over 200, and it should have blown her away, but it did nothing. Butch had protected this place from it.

His massive figure stood in front of her, the black cloth draped over him. As she drew closer, the strong scent of salt nearly overwhelmed her, burning her nostrils. He gestured to the monolith, and the sounds that erupted from him hurt her, digging into her mind.

Fear filled her. The cacophony, the inhuman noises, the obelisk, Butch himself, the storm, the voidborn, they each in turn weighed on her and her shoulders slumped from the weight. Fear had pushed her to come here, fear of the water, the terrible threat of an uninhabitable Earth, and now that terror stood in front of her.

Waves of overwhelming dread swept through her, and tears rose in her eyes.

Moira squeezed her fists, and took a deep breath, and exhaled, and breathed out. She breathed out the fear, the terror.

No. The fear was still there.

But she would use it. She would channel it. The fear would be transformed, into rage. Into action. She gripped the knife hard in her hand, and stared at the back of Butch as gnarled sounds came from his throat.

She gave him no warning, jumping onto his back and stabbing him in the neck, forcing the knife in as hard as she could, the blade cutting deep into his flesh. She swiveled and pulled out and reared back to stab him again, but he twisted to throw her, reaching over his shoulder and tossing her forward.

She flew through the air and fell onto the sandy ground. She pushed herself to her feet, ignoring the pain that ripped through her from the fall. Moira still had the knife, and she held it out in front of her. She had stabbed him in the neck, deep, and she had hit the carotid. He'd bleed out in minutes, and this would all be over.

Butch stood in front of her, the obelisk considering them both, alien and silent. Butch didn't bother holding the wound in his neck, blood pouring from it in terrible amounts. It dripped down onto his robe, staining the dark fabric. But he stood, unaffected, and then she watched as the flow slowed, and then stopped. Butch stared at her and smiled.

A real smile, a terrible one, no ounce of pretense or performance. This was the real Butch, the real Archibald, the real Ben, every other alter ego he'd ever carried. This was the true him, a massive evil grin that threatened to overtake his face, ten thousand gleaming teeth.

"Oh, Ms. Bell," he said. "You are formidable. It is always the ones you least expect. Thought you were another *snoop*, coming to pry into my business. But you are much more than that. If I had known you had communed with The Master, I would have gone about this all differently.

Maybe you'd standing here with me, instead of against."

"I won't let you do this," said Moira. She held the blade out, but after seeing him heal her previous wound so quickly, it felt like a butter knife in her hand. Her threat felt empty.

"Oh, Ms. Bell," said Butch. "You are already much too late. Do you expect to stop me with that?" He looked at the knife and laughed. A deep, horrible laugh, an inhuman laugh, its very presence enough to spark that sudden, deep rage in Moira, and she charged him. He seemed surprised again, and she stabbed upward into his abdomen, over and over again, the blade not deep enough to get to his heart, his massive size his advantage. He could heal one wound, but maybe not a dozen. She stabbed, over and over, cutting holes in his black robe, slicing into his flesh repeatedly.

Then his arms wrapped around her, and she realized she had fallen into his trap. He squeezed her hard, wrapping her in a bear hug, and she couldn't move. She couldn't breathe.

He picked her off the ground, and she kicked and struggled, but his massive size was impossible to overcome. He stared at her as she struggled, her breath gone, her ribs straining. She dropped her knife, unable to hold it anymore. All she saw was his smile as he brought her close.

"It is a pity you will not see Him awaken," said Butch. "You will not see this new world." His voice was changed now, deep, dark, and devoid of emotion. He had dropped the performance. No need now, not anymore. Now he could be who he truly was, a lieutenant for The Great Beast.

Moira tried to breathe, but her lungs were squeezed empty, and his smile filled her vision, all she could see. She kicked limply, but they did nothing. She was losing strength, and spots danced in her eyes. This is how she would die.

Not like this.

She reared back and headbutted him in the nose, and it broke with a loud CRACK. She reared back and hit him again, and again, smashing his nose into oblivion. Moira didn't know if she could kill him, but she sure as hell could hurt him. His grip weakened, and then he dropped her, and she tumbled to the ground, taking deep breaths. Butch grabbed his ruined nose.

"You bitch," he said. "Fine."

Moira scrambled to grab her knife, but Butch kicked it away, it scrabbling across the wet sand, and stomped toward her. Moira tried to crab walk away, but he was on her, his ruined nose no longer bleeding. She kicked at him, but he ignored her, grabbing her by the wrist, and dragging her across the ground. She struggled and booted him, digging her fingernails into his arm, trying to pull away, but his strength was unassailable.

"No getting away from this, Ms. *Bell*," he said, emphasizing his false southern accent with her name, another construction. "It is inevitable."

He pulled toward the obelisk, to the dark pool that lay at its base, that despite the wind and the rain, still sat calm and undisturbed. Moira kicked at him, but it did nothing, each strike bouncing off.

They reached the edge of the pool, the obelisk leaning down over them, and Butch grabbed her with his other hand, his catcher's glove mitt sized palm seizing the back of her neck, and then grabbing the front of her neck with the other.

"You'll see, now," said Butch. "You'll be welcomed into his embrace. It's easy. You'll understand." He pushed her toward the pool, the black liquid showing no reflection, the smell of salt and blood strong now, a dark chemical that would swallow her whole and transport her to the embrace of the Sleeper and its Servants. She would become one of those things, a mindless clone, an echo of herself that would serve Butch and his Master.

She pushed back with all her strength, but she had nothing to contest his might. The surface of the darkness grew closer, and closer, and she closed her eyes, waiting to be enveloped.

"I swear to God, you motherfucker," said a voice, and Moira opened her eyes to see Joan running at them and swing a crowbar, hitting Butch square in the face, right in his ruined nose with a dull, terrible THUNK.

Butch let go of Moira and she fell back, away from the pool, trying to catch her breath. Joan didn't look to her, her attention only on Butch. She swung the crowbar again, aiming for his head, this time with the sharp point. It hit him in the back of the head, digging in with a dull, meaty THUD, and he fell back with a moan.

Joan didn't stop, swinging repeatedly, as Butch did his best to cover up. She yelled as she swung at him, her big frame swinging the crowbar as hard as she could.

"You motherfucker!" she said. "You took Bill from me! You took him, and now he's gone! We had years, left! Years! And you took them from me! And now you'll pay, you piece of shit!"

She swung again and again, massive pieces of flesh carved from Butch's head, his arms, his shoulders, the crowbar digging giant divots into his body. Joan swung, over and over, her thick shoulders working hard. She screamed a final time and swung right into his face, aiming for his eye, away from his guarding hands.

THOOK.

The point of the crowbar destroyed his eye and sunk into his eye socket, the orbital bone breaking with a terrible CRACK. Joan tried to pull it back out, but it was caught in the gap.

Butch laughed, a terrible noise erupting from his throat.

He spit, a wad of blood and tissue and teeth shooting out of his mouth, and he continued to laugh, as he reached and grabbed the crowbar with his own hands, and then stood, the weapon embedded in his skull. His face was a bloody mess, but Moira saw his smile, and he ripped the crowbar out of his skull with a SHOONK and pulled it away from Joan before slamming her in the face with it with a quick motion that Moira couldn't track. Joan fell backward, cradling her face, blood pouring out from between her fingers.

"Not enough," he said, breathing through blood. "The center of the storm will be here soon. This will be *over*, soon." He was unrecognizable now, one eye peering out from a crimson mask, and he walked back toward Moira, who still sat on the ground near the pool. Moira glanced at Joan, and Joan had brought more than the crowbar with her. She had a package strapped to her back. The bomb.

Joan rolled over and looked to Moira, pulling the bomb off. She nodded to Moira, her face a bloody mess.

"Go," she mouthed.

Moira scooted herself backwards, away from the obelisk, toward the outer ring of the space, toward the ring of torches. Butch stepped after her, the crowbar dripping with both his blood and Joan's.

"What did you think you could do, Ms. Bell?" asked Butch. "I've seen things that would drive a man mad. I've learned magicks that have prolonged my life. I've cast wards that have protected me, and Blackwell Key. You're just some reporter. I've seen them come and go before. You won't be the first to fail."

Moira needed him to keep talking. "Go fuck yourself. You're a shell, a puppet for that thing you worship. You're doing this to be some monster's pet. Is that worth the whole world?"

Butch smiled, wide again, blood spilling from his mouth.

"Of course."

The rain stopped then; the wind ceased its blowing. Moira looked up, the eye wall passing over them. They were in the eye of the storm now.

"It's time," said Butch.

She still scooted backwards, and she was past the ring of torches now. Thirty feet from Joan, who held the bomb in her hands. She fiddled with wires. The ground sloped down, and water rushed up to the edge. Whatever protection the obelisk gave from the storm was not enough to keep the water out. She stood up, at the edge of the ocean. Moira glanced at Joan, who was looking at her, waiting.

Joan gave her a final nod.

Moira didn't wait, turning and diving into the water, swimming as deep as she could.

The bomb exploded behind her.

30

The bomb exploded above the surface, and Moira heard it, a massive noise, but she more felt it, a wave of incredible concussive force rolling through the water. It punched her hard in the chest, and she thought for a moment that she would die, all the air driven out of her, but then the sound of the explosion vanished, replaced with the same eerie quiet that was there prior.

She surfaced, to see the damage.

The torches remained lit, somehow, maybe a part of Butch's magic, but everything else was destroyed. The Obelisk was gone, and the pool of dark liquid had vanished as well, only a crater remaining. Moira scanned for any sign of Joan, for any sign of her remains. But the blast had obliterated her. The torches remained, as did pieces of the obelisk. A few distorted chunks of iron were strewn around the blackened sand. One other thing remained.

Butch.

His body was near where she had left him, forced back a few feet. He laid on the ground, his corpse a blackened mess. The explosion had blown off one of his arms at the shoulder, the other gone at just above the elbow. Both his legs were gone, probably taken out by shrapnel from the bomb and the obelisk itself.

Moira took a deep breath. With the obelisk gone, and Butch dead, it was over.

And then a sound rang out through the space, in the eye of the storm, the hurricane spinning around them.

Moira recognized it.

It was laughter. Butch's laughter.

He laid back, limbs missing, his body a wreck, and he laughed. He somehow still lived.

She walked over to his torso, bellowing laughter as he bled out onto the ground. He wasn't dead, not yet. He stared up at her with one eye, a bright white in a blackened face.

"Oh, Ms. Bell," he said, still smiling. "You are formidable." Moira wanted to stomp on that smile, to drive her heel right into what remained of his teeth, to force them down his throat. But she couldn't. Not yet. Her reporter's instincts remained.

"What's so funny?"

"The others were right," he said. "For so, so long. They had told me that this would never work. That this was the wrong way of going about things. That it was a moonshot. That I should be more patient. And they were right, but for the wrong reasons. I overcame every single criticism of theirs. I converted the whole town. I bid my time, and the hurricane came, and I drew it here. They didn't think I could do it, you see. No one had mastered all the different magicks. But I did it all. But *that* was their doubt. There was no concern about an outsider coming in. The others—they had never thought about it. And neither had I. And here we are."

"What others?" asked Moira.

Butch stared at her for a moment, with his one good eye, and his torched face became confused, before he laughed again, even harder, hard enough to cough, uproarious, uncontrollable laughter.

"Oh, Ms. Bell," he said. "I cannot believe it. I really cannot. Here, at the end, at least you've provided me with a little bit of joy, as hard as it is."

"What others?" she asked again.

"Did you really think I did all of this alone?" he asked.

"I saw," said Moira. "Down there in the water. I saw you drown. And I saw you come here, to prepare. Houseboat found the journal, of your friend. He died, killed himself. You have no allies. You only have your Servants."

"So you really are just a reporter?" asked Butch. "Nothing else?" He laughed again. "Certainly, we lost people along the way. Attrition is natural with any effort. Some people will be lost. But I am a single spoke on a great wheel, Ms. Bell. One of many. Did you think it was me alone that warmed the planet, to welcome our Master? No, of course not. I am but a single man, as powerful as I might be. Now, if dozens of men, all situated in positions of power, leaders, politicians, and icons of industry—if all those men spent decades working at conflating profit with destruction—then, perhaps, we could warm the Earth enough for his arrival. Maybe then." He smiled, again, wide, as what he said rolled through Moira's mind.

"You think you've stopped us?" asked Butch. "Maybe today. Perhaps you have forestalled our victory. But I wasn't lying, Ms. Bell. It is inevitable. Soon, our Master will awaken, and transform the land." He laughed again. Moira stared.

She only had one answer for him, as the anger and rage flowed through her at the thought of his will. Moira did not know if he told the truth. But she thought of the hundreds of people over the years in Blackwell Key, replaced by horrible monsters. Of Houseboat, of Mike, of Joan, killed.

Moira grabbed Butch by his robe, what still hung on him, and dragged him across the ground.

"What are you doing?" he asked, leaving a trail of blood behind him.

"I know that you've failed today," said Moira. "You've failed your Master."

"He will understand," said Butch. "He will see my great effort—"

"You can plead your case when you see him," said Moira, and pulled the body of Butch into the water. He bobbed there for a moment, but could do little to stop her.

"What? No—" he started, and then she flipped him face down, and grabbed a fistful of hair, and held him there. He screamed underwater, everything else quiet except for the faint sound of wind and some stray rain. He screamed, bubbles coming up to the surface. Butch struggled, but all his strength was gone, gone with the obelisk.

    Moira held him until he was still.

    And then for a few minutes more.

31

Moira left the body in the water. She looked up to see the eye wall. The hurricane was still there, its great winds swirling around her. Soon it would push through and engulf the island.

She heard coughing noises from behind her, coming from the water, and in her mind's eye she saw Butch again, charred but regenerating, with fresh arms and legs, coming to kill her, and her heart jumped into her throat, but then she looked, and saw a familiar figure stumble out of the sea, coughing up water.

Houseboat.

He wore a life jacket. She had seen him grab for it. It had saved his life.

"I heard the explosion," he said, after coughing again.

"Where's Butch—oh." He looked over to the floating corpse of what remained of him. He looked to Moira. "Did Mike or Joan—"

Moira stared at him and only shook her head.

Houseboat nodded, and forced tired legs over to her, hugging her. She hugged back, both of them beaten and wet. Houseboat let go, looking over what was left of Dagger Key. An expanse of sand. A few burning torches. He looked at the storm. It slowly moved in on them.

"Not looking good," he said. "But at least we killed Butch. We stopped him, right?"

Moira looked at him. "Butch said—"

"What?"

"He said he was a part of a bigger picture," said Moira. "That the cult—the worship of whatever dwells beneath the waves—it's not just him, not just Blackwell Key. He made it sound like it was everywhere. That they've been doing this for generations. Preparing for its arrival."

Houseboat stared at her, his long hair hanging behind him. He eyed her and then smiled.

"I don't see it today, though," said Houseboat. "I think that's enough for now."

The eye wall was pushing closer and closer.

"What do we do?" asked Moira. "We'll die up here on open ground. The water's worse."

Houseboat took off his life jacket and dropped it on the sand with a wet thud. "Don't think it'll do me too much good anymore. We could probably lay flat here. Dig ourselves a small trench. Hope the water doesn't raise anymore."

Moira sighed. The storm had destroyed any shelter on

Dagger Key. "I don't have high hopes—"

A crashing noise interrupted her from the shore, near Butch's corpse, and another jolt of fear ran through her. But Butch remained dead, his body floating in the water.

Something had crashed into the shore.

"Darling!" yelled Houseboat, running over to it. But it wasn't Darling, at least not all of her. The waves had torn her apart, but a piece of her hull had been pushed ashore, upside down. "Saves us again. Here, Moira. Give me a hand. We can use it as shelter."

"Will it be enough?" asked Moira.

"Always a good question," said Houseboat. "But I don't have the answer. Let's see if we can drag it ashore." Houseboat pulled the piece of hull ashore, pushing it with his shoulder. Moira joined him. It was heavy, but it slid through the sand easily enough.

"Over the crater," said Moira. "It might protect us there."

The eye wall had reached the edge of the island now, and the wind kicked up sand, the rain blowing onto them.

"Hurry!" yelled Moira. The saltwater already stung her eyes as it swirled through the air. They pushed hard, the piece of hull digging into the wet sand, but it still moved, and they pushed as hard as they could with aching backs and strained shoulders. Moira's thighs burned as she pumped them through the sand, her injuries piling up. But she still pushed.

What was left of Darling slowly slid through the sand as the storm wall pressed in on them. The blackened sand cracked as the hull broke through it, and then it was in place, and Moira and Houseboat crawled underneath the piece of ship.

Houseboat grabbed the piece of wood from below and pulled it down, putting all of his weight into it. Moira joined him as the storm moved over the island with full force. Moira's body ached as they held the hull down over them, salt water dripping down her face. Her guts ached with fear and anxiety, and worry, and grief, as the wind whipped against the side of the wood.

Houseboat stared at her, holding onto the wood with all his strength. The rain pelted it, machine gun fire on the outside.

But the hull held, with no way for the wind to get underneath and lift it. Houseboat slowly let go, and Moira did the same, and the piece of boat held still.

Houseboat fell to his butt, leaning back against the wood. Moira eased down onto her seat.

"One last favor from the girl," said Houseboat. He patted it.

A gust of wind hit the side, and it shook, but stayed put.

"I think we're okay," said Houseboat. "We just have to wait out the storm. It'll take a few hours."

"But what after that?" asked Moira. "Those things—they're still out there. And what Butch said. He wasn't lying. There are men, high-up, who want to bring The Beast here. I—"

Her hands went to her face. She wiped the salt off. She looked to Houseboat. "I don't know. After the storm—how do we defeat something so big?"

Houseboat's voice cut through the dimness underneath the hull. "I don't think we answer that yet. But I imagine we do what we did here, again and again, until we die or we win."

"I guess you're right," said Moira. She took a deep breath. "I'm so fucking exhausted."

"I'm not sure I've ever been more tired in my entire life," said Houseboat. "Hell, even after my wedding I wasn't this tired."

"Didn't know you were married," said Moira.

"Well, I was. It's a long story," said Houseboat. "I'll save it for a better time."

"Fair enough," said Moira. Rain pelted the shelter. Wind hit it, but it stayed put, and Moira's guts eased. A thought entered her mind, and she smiled.

"I just thought of a different problem," said Moira.

"Oh?" asked Houseboat. "What's that?"

"Well," said Moira. "Your boat's gone. I doubt we'll ever find any more of it, aside from what's above us."

"Yeah, you're right," said Houseboat. "I'm a man without a country."

"It's a bigger problem than that," said Moira.

"What am I missing?" he asked.

"You'll need a new name," said Moira, and started laughing, softly at first, and then louder, even as the rain and wind hit the outside of the hull, and the storm raged around them.

Houseboat was silent, and then started laughing too, louder and louder.

The storm raged around them, and they laughed, even as the sound of the maelstrom overwhelmed it.

Sign up for your free, exclusive novel!

Sign up for Robbie's newsletter! Monthly sneak peeks at upcoming projects, cover teases, and instant access to a free, exclusive novel!

www.robbiedorman.com/newsletter

Acknowledgements

Thank you to my wife Kim, for her patience and support. Thank you to my team of beta readers; Andrew, Matt, Megan, and Yousef, for your guidance and help. Thank you, for reading.

About the Author

Robbie Dorman believes in horror. What Dwells Beneath the Waves is his ninth novel. When not writing, he's podcasting, playing video games, or petting cats. He lives in Texas with his wife, Kim.

You can follow Robbie on Twitter @robbiedorman

www.ingramcontent.com/pod-product-compliance
Lightning Source LLC
Chambersburg PA
CBHW020818200625
28423CB00017B/68